CW01429543

MINION

BOOK 1:
THE SHUDAGON TRILOGY

JUSTIN TREECE

iUniverse, Inc.
Bloomington

Minion
Book 1: The Shudagon Trilogy

Copyright © 2011 by Justin Treece

All rights reserved. No part of this book may be used or reproduced by any means, graphic, electronic, or mechanical, including photocopying, recording, taping or by any information storage retrieval system without the written permission of the publisher except in the case of brief quotations embodied in critical articles and reviews.

This is a work of fiction. All of the characters, names, incidents, organizations, and dialogue in this novel are either the products of the author's imagination or are used fictitiously.

iUniverse books may be ordered through booksellers or by contacting:

iUniverse
1663 Liberty Drive
Bloomington, IN 47403
www.iuniverse.com
1-800-Authors (1-800-288-4677)

Because of the dynamic nature of the Internet, any web addresses or links contained in this book may have changed since publication and may no longer be valid. The views expressed in this work are solely those of the author and do not necessarily reflect the views of the publisher, and the publisher hereby disclaims any responsibility for them.

ISBN: 978-1-4620-7049-7 (sc)
ISBN: 978-1-4620-7047-3 (e)
ISBN: 978-1-4620-7048-0 (dj)

Library of Congress Control Number: 2011961649

Printed in the United States of America

iUniverse rev. date: 1/25/2012

ACKNOWLEDGMENTS

Illustrations	Book Cover Art	Editing
Dusty Moore	Todd Clark	Dana Micheli
	Cory Freeman	

Meike Schmidt
Jason Zaderaka

Thank you for lending me your ears, offering your thoughts, and doing what great friends do – share.

.

PROLOGUE

JERUSALEM
1010 A.D.

The laborious breaths pumping from his chest nearly masked the foot scuffing as he bustled through the dust. The sandals on his wrinkled feet churned up a ghostly cloud that trailed him through the dark city. Scattered street lamps threw his galloping shadows on alleys, sealed-shut wooden doors, and windows.

"Please save us," he whispered to the dark.

No one heard his plea. And if they did, there was no answer to his call.

"Lord, save us all from him!" He cried into the chill of the night with his hand clutching a rosary.

In his frantic stride, he tripped on the ends of his long, filthy cloak and plunged onto the bald earth.

He was not quick to his feet, and as he lay there under his smoky trail of dust, a piercing scream bounced off the walls near his side; the scream of a woman in genuine terror. The cry of a grown man followed. Both voices came from a considerable distance; both drained the clergyman of his hope.

Despite his potential injuries, he pulled himself to his feet and continued on.

"Please, please," he drooled, as the words fell from his sweat stained face.

More cries filled the air, strengthening his pace. He rounded a well-lit corner and made his best sprint towards the towering cathedral before him. He rammed into the wooden double doors with his nimble shoulder. The entrance into the cathedral was thrown wide open allowing the chill from outside to enter. The candles that were spread throughout the hall danced with the fresh air, tossing fragments of light up to the blackened ceiling above.

"Father!" a voice from the altar yelled.

"We have him Father!" another voice added.

The priest pressed on between the pews and candle stands to approach the four men awaiting him in front of the altar. With thick twine, the four peasant men were detaining a fifth man.

"Do not strike him. Under no circumstance are you to take his life!" the priest ordered.

"But we must end this father," one of the brown-skinned peasants spoke in a much more reserved tone.

"You will all be damned. Your souls marked for eternity! The last of our wishes is to feed this fire," the priest threatened.

"You are already damned. All of you!" The detained man jerked his neck, tossing his torn, black hood from his pale face to howl at the priest.

Another peasant, a blacksmith dressed in only loose pants, yanked on the rope tied around his prisoner's neck. The tug pulled the short, bald detainee to his feet. In sharp agony, the prisoner's mouth opened wide to expose a cluster of neglected teeth and to emit a crackly whine.

"Silence, butcher," a portly farmer said as he stabbed at the prisoner with a staff.

"Enough!" the priest commanded.

The priest, still clutching the rosary, pulled back the sleeves of his robe and approached the prisoner. Every inch of holiness he embodied trembled as he reached out to touch the prisoner's shoulder.

"My son," the priest began.

"My name is Warad," the prisoner's words slivered through his lips, underneath his long nostrils.

"End this, now! You know not what you will become. An eternity of agony awaits."

"Oh, but you are misled. You have yet to open those eyes, holy man."

"You must ask the Lord for his forgiveness,"

"Never."

The structure above shook as if the ground below churned. Each of the men had to search for balance to remain upright.

The tallest of the peasants stepped forward, "It is he! He comes to finish the devil's work. Let us kill this monster!"

"No. Preserve your faith in the Lord. His greatness will end this by His own means," the priest stretched out a placating hand to the peasants. The four peasants crouched as the walls of the cathedral began to shake violently. The dim candle light showed a crack progressing throughout the upper portion of the ceiling. Sounds from the walls grew louder as the black crack stretched from side to side of the massive structure.

"We must leave here, now!" one of the peasants urged.

Without warning, the ceiling of the cathedral cracked, releasing itself from the walls and soared into the cloudy night's sky. A gust of cold wind poured into the remains of the cathedral and extinguished all but a few scattered candles. As if the darkness had clamped their mouths shut, no one spoke. The four peasants released their hold on the prisoner and quietly stepped backwards, fearful of what might happen next. While Warad seemed delighted by the spectacle before him, the priest quivered and pinned himself against a wall.

A peasant pointed to the open doorway, "The Dark Son comes! There, the doorway!"

The priest turned to see a man, dressed in a smothering, black hood, standing motionless. The only flesh visible from the caped man was the lower half of his hairless face, from his broad nose to his square chin. The man's lips were pressed shut.

The priest gasped and turned, taking a hard step into Warad.

"Beg for his forgiveness. You must," the priest's voice was only slightly more present than a whisper.

"I shall only beg the true Lord to deliver your pathetic soul to MY kingdom for all time," Warad spoke nose to nose with the priest.

With a long stride, the hooded man passed through the doorway and down the center aisle. As he passed each row, the pews caught fire, filling the room with towering flames and instant, escalating warmth. The peasants surrendered, pinning themselves against the wall behind the altar. Warad, never retiring his grin, dropped to worship on his knees. The hooded man stopped his calm stride within a few paces of the priest, his face still pointed at the ground before him.

The tallest of the peasants made an outburst that stole the priest's attention. In that instant, the priest questioned his surroundings and searched for the source of the horror the peasant faced.

Inside the mind of the tall peasant, false illusions interrupted his thoughts. The holy inferno he stood in transformed into a dreary ballet of shadows. A frail creature with dangling teeth and ragged claws climbed over the burning pews with its crystal eyes fixed on the peasant himself. Multiple versions of this grey, shaved monster appeared from each dark crevice. All of them ignored everyone and everything, except for him. The creatures surrounded the peasant, taunting him with charging claws and wide open, glossy fangs. Unable to distinguish illusion from reality, he could do nothing but express his horror with endless cries.

The blacksmith slid down the wall behind him and latched on to both of his own legs. His eyes bulged and his mouth hung open wide. His face twitched as he gazed about the fiery ruins. But he was not exploring the burning, broken cathedral. He saw a river of blood and innards driving down the walls and over the floor, splashing up against him. Brains, ribs, and half eaten cattle floated by. His allies had turned to disarranged piles of rotted organs and skin tissue that were tossed through the red current. A human skull, with fragments of the tissue still attached, floated to him and nestled at his side.

The mouth of the skull opened and spoke," Betrayal."

Another of the peasants shrieked in horror along with his two brothers. Alone and in another reality, he fought a ten foot knotty, reptilian monster that transformed out of the very spear he held in his hands. The creature clawed and bit at him relentlessly. There was no defense against the massive beast that continued to grow as it attacked.

At the other side of the room, the last peasant lay on his chest, digging his feet and fingernails into the ground, inching forward. With tears pouring from his eyes, he turned his neck and looked up to see the world falling down upon him. Lava-drenched walls toppled over him along with burning trees and razor thorns. He felt his body being crushed by the burning earth, suffocating him. There was nowhere for him to escape. No hope ahead. Only death.

The priest, standing tall and cold, did not experience any of the anguish his beloved servants did, yet he quivered as he looked upon the four men, daunted by their behavior. These four men, whom he had known to be the bravest in the city, seemed to be plagued by an unseen entity, for neither the fires, the disappearance of the ceiling, nor the hooded gentleman standing motionless were worthy of such maddened responses. Their minds have gone astray, the priest thought. The priest grabbed Warad by the collar and pulled him close.

"Do you see them? Do you hear the cries of grown men? This will be your fate as well," the priest barked. Warad only laughed, ignoring the priest's words. "Save yourself from an eternity of misery," the priest whispered into Warad's grinning face.

"I shall rule my OWN eternity. The world shall call upon me

to end THEIR misery. My kingdom awaits," Warad laughed at the clouded sky above.

"You have no idea how pow-" Warad continued his rant, but stopped mid-phrase.

The brightness of the flames was instantly overturned by a consuming, white haze that stretched for an eternity. Alone, Warad peered around the heavenly luminescence, searching for meaning. Nothing but white surrounded him, until the shackles appeared around his legs and arms. Thick, polished-silver chains attached to the shackles stretched his limbs to the maximum his joints would sustain. The other ends of the chains disappeared into the white nothing. In front of Warad, a figure emerged. An elderly man, dressed loosely in the same white hue that smothered them, approached Warad holding a cane.

"Finally. I have waited for quite some time," said the bearded old man.

Warad's grin had gone sour and was replaced with a look of confusion.

"Warad, you have been punished by man ever since you could walk. No good has come from this. But we, here, have not given up hope," the hopeful old man smiled.

"What do you mean? Where are we?"

"We shall take all the time we need to cure you of your sin."

As the old man declared his plans to a shocked and appalled Warad, hundreds of soft, clean hands appeared from all angles. These hands reached for him, stroking him, grasping every inch. The gentle fingers grabbed a strong hold of him and pulled him downwards. He looked down to his feet as they sunk into the white.

"This cannot be! I was promised!"

The sinking steadily progressed and in seconds the lower half of his body was gone. The gentle strokes of the hands escalated into a rigorous and uncomfortable molestation.

"Impossible!"

Warad's chest disappeared into the white and only his bound hands, neck, and head remained before he let out his final cry.

"Lord, forgive me. Save me!"

The white haze vanished in an instant. The broken cathedral reappeared before Warad, who had his arms stretched widely in the air for no earthy reason. The fires died. The screams from the four men ended. The room went silent.

As the four peasants rose to their feet, the priest went to his knees, thanking God.

"No," Warad whimpered.

The hooded man stumbled backwards into a smoking pew. He reached out his hand as if to cast some form of supernatural spell.

Nothing happened.

He pulled himself off of the pew and ran towards the door of the cathedral.

One peasant picked up a candle stand and followed the hooded man, crying war as he hunted. The other three followed.

Warad bent over, sobbing violently.

ZEPAR

PHILADELPHIA
2011

Bent over and sobbing violently, Jack Kootz, known as "Budge", was pleading with every unattainable promise he could conjure up. His arms were bound behind his back and his knees dug into the concrete slab that supported the dock. The wooden structure above creaked as the tide rolled in.

"I didn't kill her, man! I swear it! It wasn't me. I told you who it was, the guy who hired me. But I didn't kill her, man. She was already dead!" Budge bawled to the man standing over him.

"Why should I believe you? When I meet your employer, isn't he going to tell me the same thing about you?"

Jack Kootz was a low-level thief, driver, errand boy for the wicked. His pointless existence only provided him with a meth addiction and mountains of debt. Like every scrawny thug like himself, his pale skin and cheap leather caused most to avoid him at all costs. The ones that were forced to deal with him could only hope for quick and painless business.

"Jesus man! How the fuck should I know? Didn't the cops and the doctors check her out? I know they found spunk on her, man."

"Yes they did," the man sounded disgusted, standing in the shadows cast by the moon.

"Well it can't be mine, man! You're a doctor. You took my blood. Can't you see it wasn't me?"

"That doesn't mean you didn't have a part in it."

2

The broad shouldered man in the dark sifted through shiny objects in a leather envelope. Throughout the conversation, he would repeatedly zip up the envelope, unzip it, and sort through the objects inside.

Budge hung his head; his body looked starved.

"Look, Doc. I can take you to this guy. I know where his boat is. No one can touch him, not even the Feds. It's like he's paid up with everyone. But he knows me. He trusts me. I can get you in."

"Yes, you've told me all about it."

Budge continued to sob. Unlike at the beginning of this relationship, theses cries were genuine and desperate.

"Please, Doc. Let me go?"

The doctor left the shadows and walked into the moonlight that crept though the support beams.

"You've taught me so much."

The doctor's unshaven face wouldn't hide his maddened eyes. He bent down to come face-to-face with Budge. The whites of his eyes glared along with his teeth. Everything else—his clothes, his hair, his hands—blended with the dark.

"My whole life has been wasted saving lives. Many like you: cowards, fiends, murderers. It took something sacred to me, something truly beautiful in this sad world, to be ripped out and discarded like rubbish for me to finally understand. To stop hiding and do what is right."

With a metallic click, a chain was locked to the bindings holding Budge's hands.

"What are you doing?" Budge asked.

The man rose above Budge and opened up the leather envelope.

"What are you doing?"

Budge looked around to see a stack of weights now chained to his own hands.

"No. Please no. Please Doc. Please?

The man above Budge seemed to be choosing from the items in the envelope.

"Don't drown me. Please don't drown me."

"Let us see if you wish for the same after this."

The doctor shoved a syringe in Budge's throat and squeezed the plunger until all of the yellowish fluid was transferred to Budge's insides. Almost instantaneously, the concoction began to take effect. Budge began to convulse. Drool and a trace of foam poured from his mouth. Pain was obvious, yet Budge could not speak to convey this experience in words.

"I wish more of your lot could witness this. Perhaps they would think twice. Perhaps they would choose a different routine. "

Budge shook violently and stared up at the doctor.

"But we will have to save the exhibition for another day. There are more pressing concerns than low-life thugs willing to do any job for a few bucks."

The doctor bent back down to Budge's level. Budge's eyes followed the doctor's, as if it was the only bodily function he still had control over.

"You've never felt this much pain before, have you?"

Budge could not answer.

"You see, the thing about physical pain—eventually it goes away and you never REALLY remember what it felt like."

Budge continued to stare at the smiling doctor.

"I must thank you sir, for teaching me the power of true pain, true emotional damage. Before you and your...employer came along, I was a naïve man, unversed in real suffering."

The doctor stood up and walked behind Budge.

"You're lucky. The end of your pain is down there," the doctor pointed at the waters below. "The end of my pain..."

With a black, steel-toed work boot, Dr. Kayden Archer pushed Jack Kootz into the sea, along with the stack of weights attached to his body.

"...won't be as easy to find."

(beep)

"Kayden, it's Grace. Where are you? Everyone is looking for you. Mom and Dad even called the cops. They came by the house and asked us all these questions. Something about money and more stuff about Cindy. I wanted to bash their faces in. Assholes. You gotta call or come home. The cops say they need you to come in and answer some more questions. I heard you went back to work. They said you came in for a day, but that was it..."

"Talk to me Kay. I need to know my big bro is gonna be okay. I know you miss her. And I know this has got to be hell, but you're gonna pull through. I know it. You're the strongest person I know. I love you, Kay. Please call me."

(beep)

Kayden Edward Archer checked his voicemail for what he believed to be the last time, then chucked his phone into the sea. The police would be looking for him and hiding from the authorities was not a skill he had yet practiced. A few days prior, the law was of no threat to him. Like most, following the laws of man was a duty; those who lived opposed to this idea were either fools or cowards.

Nothing seemed to fit, Kayden thought as he stood on the secluded dock. The rusted bridge and the deflated bumpers contributed to the overall decrepit condition of the dock. Not a place of glamour, yet a glorious yacht was already tied off when Kayden arrived.

The sun wouldn't be up for another hour and there was no overhead light for the men loading the ship to maneuver in. A few of the shady looking characters held flashlights in their mouths. The obvious head of operations could have helped to light the path for his crew, but instead he kept watchful eye on them with a hand on a pistol.

"Day will be here soon, let's hurry it up!" the head of security told the laborers.

Crates of supplies were being shuttled to and from the lower decks of the ship. The sweating men brought in food, booze, and other sealed cargo. For Kayden, getting this gig was easier than it should have been. He simply told the crew he was one of Budge's guys and he was there to fill in. No one bothered to question him. He somehow fit in instantly. They hadn't even considered that Budge was spending the morning at the bottom of the sea.

Fueling his hate, Kayden couldn't help but notice the genuine luxury of the ship. The décor, the comfort, the amenities were all of unique design. The price-tag for the vessel was, no doubt, in the millions. On his way back out to the pier, Kayden stopped to look at a painting hanging on the marble wall. The portrait was of a stone faced gentleman surrounded by a dozen admiring women on their knees, gawking at him lustfully. The work spoke to Kayden as if to represent superiority of men over women.

"The Maven," a voice from behind him spoke.

Kayden turned around to see a Latin man wearing nothing but a lush, red robe holding a coffee mug and a cigarette. He looked half asleep, or perhaps half-drugged.

"It was a gift made for me by an admirer of mine. A pathetic man, but a beautiful artist."

The man's thick accent and friendly nature almost comforted Kayden. He could smell the oil covering his bronze skin, mixed with an exotic cologne. Kayden turned to gaze into the painting, only to maintain his composure.

The baldheaded and boxy security officer stomped into the room where Kayden and the robed gentleman stood. He marched to Kayden and stuck a pudgy pointer finger in his face.

"No one told you to stop," the big man said.

"Daro? Is that any way to treat a guest? Relax. Have your other hounds finish the job. We have a man who appreciates the arts," the Latin man said.

Daro made it obvious that he did not approve of the gesture and then left the room. The obvious commander of the vessel leaned up against a bar and sipped his coffee.

"So, Jack had better things to do this morning than honor our agreement?" he asked.

Kayden took a moment to answer. "He might have dived in a little too deep last night."

The robed man found this entertaining.

"You know why they call him Budge? Because you can convince him to do *anything*."

"I am well aware," Kayden added.

He smirked at Kayden.

"You may call me Armand. Rarely do I introduce myself with my given name. You understand, don't you friend?"

"I wish I didn't, but I do."

"What shall I call you, friend?"

"Dan."

"Dan. How very American." Armand put out his cigarette. "You see, Dan, because Jack decided not to join us today, this puts you and I in a very difficult situation. Jack was supposed to pay his debt by performing certain tasks for me. And today, I desperately need his assistance for a particular job."

Kayden nodded.

"And due to Jack's absence I am one man down. This puts quite a damper on my plans. So my beautiful friend, I must ask for your assistance on this voyage."

"It doesn't look like I have much of a choice."

"You don't. Perhaps another important bit of information Jack did not explain to you is the confidentiality I am forced to maintain with *all* of my associates. Before our business is finished Dan, you must earn my trust. Just as I should earn yours."

"I suppose I'm in. Remind me to thank Jack," Kayden had to concentrate on his tone on order to sell it.

"We can both thank him," Armand laughed. "This works out better for us all. You seem to have a better grip on your life than that junkie."

Daro trotted back in to the room with authority.

"We are loaded," Daro said to Armand, he then stepped to Kayden. "Time for you to catch up with your kind, chief."

Kayden ignored Daro.

"Dan is with us today. He's filling in for Jack," Armand told his number one.

"We don't know this mother-" Daro, frustrated, shot back.

"I said, he is with us today. Get him some gear," Armand ordered.

Daro shook his head and started to leave the room to ready the boat for departure. Before he left, he grabbed Kayden by his sweatshirt and pulled him in close.

"Don't fuck this up, or I'll put you down fast, big man," Daro whispered into Kayden's ear.

Daro exited the room to release the ship from the dock. Armand approached Kayden and patted his shoulder.

"My friend. Let us watch the sun rise on America. Today, we hunt for our keep. Tonight we celebrate as we dine on our earnings," Armand spoke to the sea. "This is freedom!"

Only a few weeks prior, Kayden had been a different man. He had a wife, a home, money, happiness. Overnight, he became a bankrupt widower. Instead of saving lives for the good of mankind, he now strove to take them.

While the rest of Armand's men slept through the morning, Kayden stared into the ocean. Part of him wanted the waters to wash away all of his grief, his torment. Part of him wanted to grab something sharp and shove it into Armand's throat as he sipped his cocktails and yakked on his cell phone. But he had to know. Questions must be answered. He forced himself to be patient.

Over and over again, Kayden replayed the events of the night his wife was killed. The first thing he remembered about the evening was surgery; another successful heart transplant. He remembered a dark spurt of blood jumped onto his face as if anticipated, for he did not flinch or blink. The assistant at his side, holding the next required device, jerked backwards and bumped into the anesthesiologist. His assistant was more nervous than usual during that very intense operation.

"Ms. Jasper?" Dr. Archer spoke, never once taking any focus off of his work.

The assistant handed him a polished utensil and took two fearful steps away from the operating table. Archer took the tool from her hand and swiftly maneuvered it inside the unconscious woman. The doctor never once took his eyes off the open innards of his patient.

"Just crossing the two hour mark, Kay," a co-worker spoke.

"Thank you, Paul" Kayden replied.

Two hours and fifty-one minutes later, he left the operating room while his colleagues sewed back his patient's incision. He hit the locker room for a hot shower. At that late of an hour in the confines of Hahnemann University Hospital, Kayden had the whole locker room to himself.

"Sooner or later you are going to have to share your secrets with the rest of the world," Paul Dansin spoke from the other side of the shower curtain.

"I don't have any secrets. Just luck," Kayden spoke loud enough to be heard over the running water.

"No. Your patients are the ones who are lucky, Kay."

"Anyone could do what I do. Many do it a lot better."

"I'm still waiting for when you wise up and get out of this place. Go somewhere nice. Start your own thing somewhere. Every fat pig in this part of the world would be at your door with bags of pesos."

"Oh yeah?"

"Absolutely."

Yanking the shower curtain to the side, Kayden covered his wet, lower body with a clean towel and opened his locker.

"Then what? Hand out corporate dope to fanatic housewives and crooks that can't get it up?" Kayden said, fumbling through a bag of toiletries.

Paul shrugged, and then laughed through his nostrils. Kayden reached deep into the locker and pulled out a stick of deodorant. A dry, folded newspaper fell from the locker and on to the damp ground. Kayden picked up the paper and starred at the front page.

"*Drug King Murders Family of Four: Only a week after extensive heart surgery, Otto Mansfield was brought into custody for the alleged murder of the Hughes family, who were found slain in their suburban home. The official report states...*"

"Why do you keep that?" Paul asked.

"To remember."

"Remember what? That some whack-job killed a family over drug money?"

"To remember that I could have stopped him."

"Kayden. You saved a man's life, like you have done hundreds of times, regardless of who he was. This is what you do. You are not a judge. It's not your job to decide who lives or dies."

"I pulled out a half-dozen bullets from this man's chest, only so he could turn around and put them back into an entire family."

"You had no clue, whatsoever, that he was going to do that. No one could have."

Kayden nodded and looked away from the paper.

"Now throw that thing away and get dressed. Me, you, and the ladies are going out for something edible. It's on me, for a change," Paul cockily yelled, clapping his hands together.

When Paul left the locker room, Kayden took another hard glance at the article before carefully placing it inside his locker. He pulled a clean white t-shirt over his brawny upper body and jammed his legs into a faded and slightly torn pair of blue jeans. The locker door slammed shut after the doctor pulled his dark overcoat and folded it over his arm.

Paul awaited Kayden just outside of the locker room, mashing the buttons on his cell.

With a hurried pace, the two walked down a bright hallway cluttered with rolling beds, some of which were empty, some occupied by patients.

"Haven't seen your kid sister around much. What has she been doing?" Paul asked.

"Still driving the folks nuts. Can't seem to stay in one dorm room for more than month," Kayden said.

"Has she decided on med-school? Be a great doctor, like her big brother?"

"I hope not."

"Why is that?"

"She doesn't need to follow my steps. She's way smarter than I'll ever be."

"Me and the missus saw her and your mother at church last weekend."

"Yes. They mentioned that."

"Where were you?"

Kayden chuckled.

"Sunday mornings, me and Cindy sleep. We send in the family to take notes and report back."

"I see. Father Randal mentioned you used to be there every Sunday morning before you married. He baptized you?"

"That he did."

"Your mother and Father Randal seemed to have quite a history."

"She is very appreciative of Father Randal. She calls him her redeemer. I'm not exactly sure why."

Kayden shook his head and smiled. A pair of engaged females in scrubs, wearing name tags and holding clipboards, rushed past Kayden and Paul. The dark-skinned nurse blurted out the name *Archer* during their conversation. Kayden stopped his pace.

"Excuse me?" Kayden called to the nurse.

"Yes?" she replied.

"I am Dr. Archer. Dr. Kayden Archer."

Her eyebrows bowed, she seemed confused.

"Yes?"

"I am sorry ma'am. I swore I heard my name. Sorry to interrupt you."

As Kayden stepped forward, the woman referenced her clipboard.

"Ah yes, you did. Archer. But not Dr. Archer. Cindy Archer. Just admitted to ER. Multiple stab wounds. ER room F5," the woman stated, pointing down the hall.

In that instant, Kayden Archer's world folded in on itself. He would later recognize that moment as the time he crossed over.

The overcoat draped over Kayden's forearm fell to the ground along with his face, yet his exhausted eyes snapped open. After a few pulsing seconds, he broke his stone gaze on the nurse and leapt down the hallway in a full sprint. Paul followed.

The numbers of the individual rooms flew passed Kayden. G3...G2...G1.

Within seconds, the sweat began to pour from his face.

F8...F7...F6.

Kayden approached the open doorway to an isolated emergency room titled F5 with Paul at his side. Frozen in time, Kayden watched as a nurse gently covered the lifeless face of a young woman with a white sheet. Archer stepped in and ripped the sheet away from the nurse's grasp and off the face of his wife. She was covered in blood, some of which had dried to her pale skin. Her clothes had been cut apart for treatment. Her face was badly beaten.

Someone screamed his name from down the hall. Kayden's bulging eyes left the body on the bed and looked down the hallway to see two nurses holding back a teenage girl.

She tried desperately to claw her way around the two nurses, screaming Kayden's name, but his slender younger sister was no match for two healthy nurses. Paul left Kayden's side to tend to the distraught youngster.

"Grace, relax. There's nothing you can do now," Paul yelled as he approached the fighting girl.

Kayden, shocked and frozen, refocused his attention to the room where his dead wife lay. His eyes flooded with tears. Kayden could barely bring himself to touch her. He knew there would be no life to feel. Shaking, he lifted her head up in his arms.

What came out of Kayden as he held his wife's body could be described as a vicious roar to the high heavens, cursing the world that God created. Everyone on the floor stopped in their tracks to listen to true horror reverberating through the halls.

Kayden did not resist and allowed his mind to replay the evening over and over again. It was his fuel, his reason. Never in his life had he desired retribution of that magnitude. After her death, he sought nothing other than diabolical revenge.

Armand broke his concentration when he joined him on the open deck. He had changed out of his robe and into an all white, loose fitting outfit. He reminded Kayden of a retired Miamian, letting his stringy hair run with the breeze.

"I see you are enjoying the view. You've been out here all morning," Armand said.

"I don't travel on boats often."

"The sea is beautiful. It will wash away all sins."

Kayden didn't respond.

"I love America. Do you know why?"

Kayden shook his head.

"The women. They are so eager to be in power. Women have maneuvered themselves into control. They have power in business, politics. Some even earn the wealth while the man stays at home to tend to the children. And they love it. Women have little battles amongst themselves to see who can acquire the most control."

"They can be persuasive," Kayden added.

"Ah, but only to the weak. We, as men, must be strong. We must demand the control."

"Easier said than done."

"To the contrary, I find it to be very simple. The key is to find out their ambitions and let them taste their own success. Once that happens, they will beg for more."

"You seem to have experience."

"Well, yes, my friend. Guilty as charged," Armand laughed. "Every man or woman has greed. And if they can stay hidden, they will betray to fulfill that greed. They just have to be given the opportunity."

"I have no doubt."

Armand stretched himself out and sipped on a cocktail. He shut his eyes and lifted his sunglasses away from his eyes, allowing the sun to smother his face.

"So how does a decent man like yourself get mixed in with a guy like Budge?"

A swarm of lies tumbled through Kayden's thoughts, but he could only think of the truth.

"He helped kill my ex," Kayden answered Armand.

"I see. Well, sometimes we need a guy like Budge to do the dirty work. If he wasn't so good, I wouldn't give him a second glance."

The day he had met Jack Kootz, aka Budge, was the day he had dragged himself out of his home and back to work for the first time after his wife's death. He surprised himself for having the strength to return to a job he was no longer interested in. Jack Kootz had been in the hospital all morning, demanding the administrative staff to let him see the doctor that authorized his heart surgery. He wanted to know why he was still in pain and he wanted answers immediately. No physician had the time or the patience to offer him, except Kayden. It wasn't normal practice for Dr. Archer to take office visits or diagnose patients. He hadn't done that for quite some time. But perhaps he felt that a little rewind to the past would be beneficial.

Kayden could see signs of serious drug abuse immediately. Jack couldn't remain still for even a moment and he poured sweat even in the controlled climate. But when Kootz removed his shirt to continue the examination, it was Kayden's own heart that nearly failed.

Mixed in with other assorted jewelry hanging from Jack's neck, was one particular item. The handmade item was a piece of bone that had been carved into the shape of a kneeling man with a horrified face. Kayden knew this item very well. It was the first gift his mother ever gave him. It had hung from a lamp in Kayden's bedroom since he was a toddler.

When Cindy and Kayden Archer moved into their first home, Kayden tried to throw the necklace out. He hated it and never knew why his mother had given him such an odd gift at such a young age. But Cindy adored the piece of jewelry. She thought it matched several outfits and probably held sentimental value of some sort. She kept it and wore it on occasion.

Kayden took back the necklace before sending Jack Kootz on his way to hell. It stayed on his neck, tucked under his shirt ever since.

After a half-day of sailing, the yacht cruised deep into a residential bay in Brigantine, just Northeast of Atlantic City. The coastline was filled with multi-million dollar properties and boat docks harboring a varied collection of sailboats and yachts. A speedboat appeared from the aft and drifted dangerously close to Armand's ship. About this time, Daro made his way to Armand and Kayden.

"Your ride is here boss," Daro stated.

"Ah, time to go to work. Dan, Daro here will fill you in on the details. You are in good hands. I will join you later this evening. I'm bringing a few friends back with me, so have Daro find you some clothes. We want to be gladiators tonight. Are you with me, my friend?"

"Sure thing."

"Excellent. Enjoy yourself, Dan."

Armand switched boats. The much smaller craft was driven by two men in dark sunglasses. Neither of them held any kind of facial expression. They left quickly.

Daro tossed Kayden a ski mask. The rest of the crew, some with binoculars, looked ahead towards a three-story estate that sat on the edge of a hill facing the water. Everyone looked enthusiastic, but Kayden didn't even try to hide the regret he had instantly felt.

"Everything?" Paul asked.

"Yeah, everything," Grace Archer answered.

"Are they sure it was Cindy?"

"Without a doubt. She setup the withdraw. Forged his signature. She even had a fake Kayden come in with a bogus I.D. to sign it out. They have video of the whole thing. Three different banks."

"I don't believe it. I can't."

"Neither did I. "

Paul crumbled up the plastic that held his lunch and tossed it in the bin. Grace only nipped at the sandwich that she had purchased from the hospital's cafeteria. Had her roommate, in the dorms of Eastern University, had acted like a civilized young adult and not a panic induced adolescent, she might have packed a lunch, as usual. Instead, after waking up to the nuisance on the other side of the room, she tied her curly hair back, threw on the only thing clean, and retreated to her home-away-from-home-away-from-home–the hospital.

"I hate cafeteria food," Grace stated.

"So she was killed the same day she made the withdrawal?"

"Yep. "

Paul paced around the break room in his scrubs. Grace nervously watched Paul float around the room.

"Kay isn't doing himself any favors taking off for days without telling anyone. Cops are looking to question him. They think he is the only one that can make any sense of this," Grace said and threw the rest of her sandwich in the garbage.

"Maybe she was threatened," Paul suggested.

"Bank teller told the cops that she seemed happy. Like she was on vacation. And that she was very touchy feely with the man she was with."

"No way. I've known Cindy for years. She would never."

"Certainly doesn't look like she was being faithful to Kayden."

"I can't even fathom this."

Grace stuck her face in her hands. Her long, hanging locks of dirty blonde hair allowed her to hide from the world. Paul sat down next to her and rubbed her back.

"He'll turn up soon. He probably just needed time to think."

"If he's not dead," Grace uttered, hunched over.

"Why would he be dead?"

"Maybe he killed himself."

"Grace, don't say that. Never say that."

"What would you do if you found out your murdered wife was cheating on you and took away everything you spent your life earning. Think of how betrayed he must feel. I wouldn't want to go on."

Paul started to reply, but didn't. He searched for words, but found none. He looked to the heavens for answers, but heard no voice. Grace surrendered her tough girl façade and let her tears flow. Paul held her tightly.

"He's going to make it. I know him. He will fight for as long as it takes," Paul offered.

Paul's phone rattled against the pens and loose change in his pocket. With the hand that wasn't comforting Grace, he grabbed the phone and checked the incoming caller ID. He immediately answered it. Loud sobbing erupted from the phone that startled both Paul and Grace.

"Baby?" Paul stood up and pressed the phone hard against his ear.

"Paul. Our son. He wasn't there. He is always there. He wasn't..."

"Calm down. Breathe. Just talk to me. Tell me what happened. "

"Our son, our little boy. He's gone. He's gone." The sobbing became more intense.

"What do you mean? Did you pick him up from school?"

"I waited for hours. I looked everywhere. Teachers, cops, everyone looked."

Paul looked at Grace. In that instant, her troubles did not

concern him. True panic took hold. He burst through the break room door and sprinted down the hall.

Grace dropped to the floor and curled into a ball.

○

In a stranger's home, Kayden couldn't continue to play the role of the hard-edged thug. While the others hacked into safes, downloaded from hard drives, and sifted through jewelry boxes, Kayden looked at family photos. He read the fine print of each diploma on the wall and rubbed his fingers on different award plaques and ornaments. The summer home he had intruded upon belonged to a successful politician.

The pictures on the walls told the story of the family. The older, lower quality, photos were of a happy couple raising three young girls. He couldn't help but think about Cindy and how she pestered him to have children. Kayden never truly humored the idea of being a father. If he were to start a family, his finances would have to be flourishing enough to give his children more opportunities than he had. Cindy never understood this. She felt that love and attention were enough to bring forth a child. She nagged him at every corner with the issue, but Kayden just changed the subject.

As the children in the photos became older, so did the parents. The lady of the family was pictured wearing either a bandana or a sunhat. She had obviously lost her hair. Several photos showed signs of the declining health of the mother, yet she still smiled in every shot. The newer, crisper photos did not include the original mother, yet displayed a new woman— an attractive brunette with a tall and proud exterior. Kayden could only assume the father remarried after his wife passed on. Something Kayden would never consider doing. The end of his marriage with Cindy had altered his approach to life enough. Trying again wasn't an option.

Kayden, suited in mostly black with a ski mask, stayed away from the others as they made haste. He gradually walked from room to room, in some way, paying his respect to the owners.

Part of him wanted the cops to show up and break up the whole operation. He would go to jail, where he could give up his campaign and just disappear for a few years. But something was making this easy. Something was aiding him on his journey. Something was clearing a path. He felt an uncomfortable sense of freedom he had never before experienced, which he allowed himself to take advantage of.

"We're done. Back to the boat," Daro yelled from the living room.

"I still have files to rip!" one of the computer thieves yelled.

"Leave it!"

Resuming their endeavor, Kayden turned away from the photos to join the escape. The small swarm of men left the home with full bags and thumb drives full of data. Most left the boat dock in an inflatable single engine craft, while Daro left on a jet ski. Kayden took one look back to see the massive home disappear along with the sun. He was the only thief without a smile or a bag of loot.

Once the party reached the yacht, the patrol boat and jet ski were lifted onboard. After securing all the valuables, the yacht vacated the area with haste. Kayden privately announced his retirement from thievery by tossing his ski mask in the water. Daro handed him a black dress shirt, black belt, a pair of dark grey slacks and ordered him to get dressed. The rest of the crew was frantically peeling off their clothes and jumping into evening outing attire. Apparently, looking good for the boss was a major concern on Armand's crime boat.

The yacht reached yet another questionable dock with no supervision and a deteriorating structure. Waiting to board ship were Armand and two slender women; a blonde and a brunette, both well groomed and dainty.

"Ahoy, men! Have a good day of fishing?" Armand asked, removing his sunglasses.

The men answered with a grunt or a nod.

Armand handed a black duffle bag to Daro. The two men met eyes and smiled.

"Okay men! Let us celebrate!" Armand yelled with two hands in the air.

The two men hollered their agreements like cheerleaders. The ship left the dock, just as quickly as it had arrived.

Kayden avoided the spotlight at any social event. Occasionally, he would give a formal speech regarding health care to fellow colleagues or students. When forced into social outings, he usually sipped one watered down cocktail for hours, smiling to friends, allowing conversation with those who wished to approach him. Comfort was something Kayden never found at any special occasion, yet nothing compared to the anguish he felt as he celebrated a robbery.

So pretending to be festive was nothing but a series of frustrating incidences. Armand nagged relentlessly at Kayden to stay on par with the crew's consumption of different wines and hard liquors. The young woman that forced herself onto Kayden's lap couldn't keep her heavily conditioned, golden hair from getting in his face. The onslaught of terrible humor and boyish duels stretched from one end of the boat to the next. The leader of this tribe danced, let his clothing hang loose, and screamed his joy to the stars. But nothing troubled Kayden more than the brunette woman at Armand's heels. Kayden knew her face from the pictures on the walls of the house they robbed earlier. In person, she was equally attractive, especially for a middle-aged woman. She sat with her legs crossed wearing a skirt long enough to cover her knees. Her smile was pearly white behind painted lips. Every time Armand would parade by, she would reach out to touch him, demanding his attention.

Kayden could barely tolerate the sight of her. It sickened him to see the look of accomplishment and control painted on her face. He forced himself to look away, pushing himself to stay in character. At the home they had robbed, the pictures on the walls showed a nurturing mother. But with Kayden's own eyes, he saw a conniving monster; a woman ridden with lust. She had sucked out her family's wealth and handed it over to Armand. She had betrayed her sacred marital vows and ducked out to a guest cabin to make love to Armand, twice during the party. She did all this with a smile.

What Kayden was looking at was his own demise manifested right before him. A greedy king, empowered by a clan of nobodies, scoured the earth for wedded scamps with a nice pair of legs and access to wealth. With his cheap and processed allure, the king convinced his newly found intermediary to leave her boring existence, take the removable assets, and join him for a life-long cruise. What the pair of legs didn't know was how short that life-long cruise may have been for them. Armand's resume did not include long-lasting relationships.

As horrid as it was to even try, Kayden couldn't see his wife on Armand's yacht, sipping wine and listening to his bullshit. He hadn't fully accepted Cindy's actions. He had accepted Armand's intentions.

The yacht sat for hours in the middle of the ocean, a few miles from the Pennsylvanian coast. One by one, the crew drank themselves to sleep. Even militant Daro ended his evening curled up on the kitchen floor snoring. The ones that withstood the night were Kayden, the two women, and Armand.

"Let's go somewhere," the blonde whispered into Kayden's ear. She had resorted to practically giving Kayden a lap dance. It was difficult to fight off the urge to shove her into the ocean.

"Let us all retreat to my room for more drinks and less clothing!" Armand offered, sweating booze.

Kayden allowed the blonde to drag him to his feet. The four of them descended to Armand's quarters. The room was much like a honeymoon suite, richly decorated and kept clean. The two women threw themselves on the enormous bed and Armand fell into the sofa on the other side of the room.

"What's wrong? You don't want to join us on the bed?" asked the brunette.

"I am sorry, I must be dehydrated. Dan! Dan my savior! Please, my friend, will you make us all a drink?" Armand sluggishly pointed to the bar in the corner.

"Certainly." Kayden agreed. He gathered three glasses and when there were no eyes on his back, he quickly reached into his pocket and retrieved an ingredient which he slipped into the cocktails. For the first time all evening, a true smile broadened Kayden's face.

The booze burned Armand's awakening eyes when Kayden poured half a bottle of vodka over his head. But neither his burning eyes nor the hand towel stuffed in his mouth was the main concern. A pain from elsewhere had stolen most of Armand's attention. It was rather unfortunate for him that his drooling screams were muffled by the towel muzzle.

"So, now you wake up," Kayden teased.

Seated in a wooden chair, Armand did not want to look at the pain. His eyes sweated tears of anguish. His pores shoved out gallons. What energy he held was used to cry for help, regardless of its hopelessness.

Armand finally grew the courage to look down at his hands. In the center of each hand, a nail, close to a half-inch wide and a half-foot long, had been driven through the flesh and into the armrests. Despite being nailed to a chair, the blood flow was oddly down to a minimum. A couple of pools had collected at the legs of the chair that had already begun by the time Armand awoke.

"I would have thought for sure you would have woken up on the second one." Kayden laughed as he spoke. He had to speak a little louder than usual to be heard over the idling engine only a few feet away. Kayden had brought them away from Armand's quarters and into a small maintenance room, where they could talk privately.

Cries for help turned to moans enriched by agony. Kayden carefully put the vodka bottle down on the hard floor and reached into his pocket and pulled out a photograph and stuck it in Armand's face, forcing him to observe. The photo was an informal headshot of Cindy.

Armand sucked it up for a couple of seconds to take a look at the picture. By his immediate reaction—a widening of the eyes and a turn of the cheek—Kayden knew the young lady was familiar to Armand.

"This is my wife. Or was, I should say. She was until," Kayden had to think about when he actually lost his wife, for he had intangibly lost her long before her death, "well, whenever you two met. Then she left me for good. I thought for sure the moment you laid eyes on me, you would put it together and we would have it out right then and there, but of course not. You don't have the time to care about whose life it is that you are destroying. All you care about is the win," there was an almost humorous tone to Kayden's delivery. He was enjoying himself.

Armand tried to communicate by mumbling. Kayden reached out and removed the gag from Armand's mouth.

"Hey! Daro! Someone! Get in here!"

"You know they can't hear you in here. Budge told me all about your little room below where you don't want to be bothered. The place where no one can hear the screams."

"Listen Dan. I...I can explain everything. Just let me...let me find a way to explain."

"My name is not Dan. It is Kayden. Kayden Archer. You remember the name, right? Cindy Archer?"

"Listen to me, Dan. I—I'm not your guy. It wasn't me. Get these things out of me, Dan!" Armand could barely talk.

"How much of this boat do I own, Armand? How much of what she gave you paid for all of this? I am curious."

"It wasn't me. I swear it. I would never—"

"You would never? And what happened today? Was that not your doing? Stealing from a man, using his wife to help you. Oh no, you would never."

After Kayden had called him out on his bullshit, Armand gave in. Armand actually started to laugh. The kind of insane giggle a coked out lunatic would project. He let go of his cowardly retreat and went back to being himself.

"I would. I do. I do it all the time. It's my thing." Armand could barely spit the words through his half drunk, half wise guy chuckling.

At last, Kayden could lean back and allow the truth to reveal itself.

"Men like you, who are slaves!" Armand almost exploded from his seat, roaring at Kayden. "You let these women walk all over you. Carry *you* around like dogs...DOGS! You are all cowards! You are more like mice than dogs."

"And what are you Armand?" Kayden calmly asked.

"I am the last hope. The only one, I see, who is not scared to take a seat at the throne. To take from the world what is mine and leave the scraps for the weak. I'm the only one carving his mark in the stone. I am what man was until...the woman stuck her face out of the window, spying on matters that did not concern her. "

Kayden shook his head and smiled. "So, keep them chained up in the bedroom, huh?

"Why not! When they get out, what do they do?" Armand waited for an answer. Kayden didn't even humor him. "They do what is natural to them. They find another bedroom to chain themselves to. "

If his chest had not caved in from Armand's words, Kayden might have been able to hold his smile. Regardless of his disagreement, the reality of his wife's deceit finally began to settle in.

"Only now, they have the key to unlock themselves. They can walk about and whore their way into power. With no hesitation, they can spend a man's wealth as if they earned it themselves. I see men who have allowed their wives to put chains on them!"

"If you are the last hope, then why destroy a man's life? Why steal?"

"If they are going to be pathetic enough to let their whore sit at the throne, then I have no sympathy. Living like a true man is not simple work. For a king, there are prices to pay; prices higher than them all. But everything has a price."

Kayden didn't respond. He stared at Armand with a glaze smeared over his face, as if he was amused and amazed by Armand's testimony.

"I should have let your wife go, so that you could see her suffer for the rest of her short life. So that she could pay for her disloyalty right before your eyes."

"Sorry, Armand, I don't get it." Kayden shook it off as if Armand was merely blurting out his last words of nonsense.

"And you can't. You are a doctor, yes? May I call you Doctor Dan?" Armand laughed, "No doctor knows the answer. I carry with me a poison, buried so deep in my blood that you can't see it. So deep that I am immune to its deadly powers."

"Right," Kayden wouldn't take him seriously.

"But the ones I take into my bed, they are never so fortunate."

Kayden did take these words to heart and mind. His focus trailed back to the days following his wife's death. He had demanded all of the conclusive data on his wife's autopsy. Although unrelated to cause of death, the physician was rather troubled by the catastrophic breakdown of her immune system and the advanced stage of deterioration in several of her vital organs. The parties involved speculated drugging or perhaps poisoning before the murder. Kayden hadn't given this much attention, until Armand's drunken profession.

"I have traveled around this world with ease. Like a prophet for the good of man. Reclaiming the throne, ridding the world of two-faced women, and placing our wives back at our feet, where they belong."

Kayden's amusement was replaced by straight-out hatred; hatred for Armand; hatred for his wife; hatred for the choices he had made; hatred for himself.

"And yes. I have done this at *your* expense."

These words sprang Kayden into action. He reached behind Armand's chair for a funnel attached to a long, riveted tube and a red, plastic tank of fuel. With no comment or hesitation, Kayden shoved the tube down Armand's throat. Gagging on the tube, he couldn't vomit, as there was not enough space in his esophagus; he could hardly even breathe.

After the tube was far enough down Armand's throat for the funnel to sit on his lips, Kayden pulled a vial from his pocket and opened the eye dropper cap. He poured the orange liquid from the vial onto the floor.

"Something to remember you by," Kayden explained as Armand's eyes began to roll back in his head.

With the eye dropper, Kayden collected the blood that oozed from Armand's hand injuries. He squeezed his collections into the empty vile, sealed it shut, and put it back in his pocket. Returning to his previous task, he picked up the tank of fuel and popped off the cap.

Armand's eyes opened and he tried to scream.

Kayden lifted the tank to head height and tipped the open cap towards the funnel. Liters of gasoline poured into the funnel in big, bronze gushes of fluid at a time. In no time, the fuel filled Armand's body to the brim, the excess seeping through his mouth.

Wasting no time, Kayden pulled a cigarette lighter from his pocket and struck the flint. Stepping back, he tossed the lighter at the funnel. A ball of flame immediately rose from Armand that reached the ceiling instantly. The screams could barely be heard over the rumbling flames. Kayden watched as Armand's body seemed to explode from the inside, his organs melting and bubbling up through his lips.

Armand's nervous system went into shock. His body convulsed in the chair madly. His legs bounced in the seat, his head twisted and turned, his arms shook so violently that they completely ripped away from the nails that kept him secured to the seat. Armand's engulfed body rose. The funnel dropped to the ground while the tube melted inside his chest. Kayden backed away into the corner.

Armand busted through the door and charged up a ramp

leading to the lounge where his employees were sleeping off their consumption. The crew was awoken by the gurgling screams and the heat of the flames smothering Armand's body. The man on fire ended up face forward on the floor, motionless.

The flames quickly spread to the carpet and furniture. With fire extinguishers, Daro and the others put out the flames cooking Armand and the rest of the yacht. There was no chance in saving Armand.

Daro looked around at each member of the crew, making a head count. He ran to the bedroom to find the two women out cold on the bed.

"Where is that Dan motherfucker?" Daro yelled. The crew left Armand's dead body smoking on the ground to search for the missing member of the crew. They searched the open deck, the kitchen, the bridge. Both auxiliary crafts were still onboard.

Daro went down the ramp and into the engine and tool room. He opened the door to find Kayden on the ground, gasping for air. Small pools of fuel were on fire. A flaming chair, right in the middle of the concrete room, would soon be a pile of ash.

Kayden was having a seizure. His face seemed controlled but his body twitched and convulsed. He tried to stand, but couldn't. Blood trickled from his nose.

"You son of a bitch!" Daro kicked Kayden while he was down, which actually deadened Kayden's shock.

Daro reached down with his thick hands and pulled Kayden to his feet by his neck. Daro squeezed on Kayden's throat with all the strength he had. Kayden gained enough control of his hands to try and pry a part Daro's grip, but it was no use. The lack of blood and oxygen turned Kayden's face blue. His legs went limp. His shoulders dropped. His arms gave up their fight.

"Die, fucker!" Daro spit in his face.

Before the end, Kayden opened up his eyes wide and looked into Daro's eyes. Kayden grinded his teeth for one final stand for his life.

By some unnatural force, Daro was thrown away from

Kayden, through the door behind him, slamming against a metal stairwell. Daro cried out loudly, in pain from several broken bones, confounded as to why he was on his back.

Kayden hit the ground coughing, but alive. He looked over to see Daro several feet away and wounded. Kayden brought himself to his feet. He stumbled over towards Daro. To gain his balance, he reached for the hand rail to the utility stairwell that Daro's injured body lay against. When he reached for the handrail, it collapsed. The steel framework bent and crumbled like tin foil.

Not able to grab onto support, Kayden staggered and rammed into an adjacent wall, yet remained on his feet. Daro watched, bewildered and horrified.

"What are you?"

Kayden, just as mystified, had no answer. His muscles twitched as he coughed. Bent over, he ascended up the ramp that led to the lounge. He was met there by a few members of the crew and Armand's dead body laying on the floor smoking.

"There he is!" one of the crew yelled. Kayden's face met with the butt of a pistol. The blow knocked him to the ground.

A kick to the ribs forced Kayden's body to curl up in agony. The crew rushed by him and down to the engine room, where they found Daro.

"Kill him. Do it now!" Daro instructed.

Delaying the order, the man who had made the bleeding gash in Kayden's face swung his leg around to kick him in the ribs once more. Just as his boot connected with Kayden's guts, the man's leg was thrown away from Kayden at an unnatural speed, launching him upside down though the lounge and crashing against the painting on the wall, knocking the thug out cold. Kayden pushed himself to his feet and forced his wobbling legs to escape. Bullets flew by as he shuffled around furniture and bodies. As he progressed through the yacht, the walls around him started to cave in. Giant sized cracks and holes formed in walls of the vessel as he ran through it. Furniture that Kayden came in close contact with was miraculously tossed around the yacht.

Kayden assumed he was hallucinating. Glass crashed into pieces all around him. The walls folded like foil. Fire danced around like rain in the wind. Nothing seemed natural. Nothing felt usual. The entire structure seemed to be moments from total collapse for no clear reason.

Kayden approached a door leading to the open deck at the furthest aft part of the ship. The instant his mind stirred the primitive idea of opening the door to proceed, the steel hinges, the trim, the locks, and the door itself burst into pieces and flew out into the ocean. Stunned, Kayden stopped at the entranceway. Another bullet whizzed by his head, snapping him out of his daze and forcing him to proceed to the open deck.

Outside, he couldn't visualize an escape. There were no other ships or land that he could swim to, especially in his condition. The lights from the coast were visible, but several dark miles away. He didn't have much time to think about it before the crew was right on top of him.

On the deck above, three men ran along the outside railway to the stern of the ship that overlooked the open deck Kayden stood at. They each held pistols. When they approached the stern, they pointed their guns at Kayden.

"Don't move, asshole!"

Kayden stood still, holding his broken ribs that swam around in his guts. He had no response, much less a rational thought. He had no earthly idea how Daro was pushed away from squeezing the life out him. No simple reason why the stairwell crumbled like a candy wrapper. How the furniture slid or flew out of his path was above him. He didn't have a clue as to why the whole place seemed to fall apart by his very existence.

Slowly, Kayden rested his hands on his head to surrender. He turned around to face the three men with guns above.

"Don't you fucking move!"

This pain in his ribs died for a few seconds as he watched the top two decks of the yacht rip apart from stern to bow and project upwards and laterally. The chunk of steel, glass, rope, and electrics that used to be the top portion of ship crashed into the sea a half-mile away, taking the gunmen with it.

Looking ahead to see the bottom half of the ship afloat, there wasn't much for Kayden to witness but destroyed furniture and the jagged edges of the remaining structure. Those light bulbs which had survived now blinked and shorted out. He could see that the satellite boat now floated unmanned along the side of the ship.

Hesitantly, two quivering heads popped out of the ruins. Both of them, blonde and brunette, were covered in ash. The two women met eyes with Kayden at the other end of the ship. The fright that had taken control wouldn't allow the ladies to call for him, regardless of how much they wanted to.

It wouldn't matter. He couldn't offer answers. There were no explanations he would possibly manufacture. Part of him wanted to take the women and run. Like them, he himself was baby steps away from a total breakdown. He backed himself into the furthest corner he could.

It only took an instant for the remaining part of the boat to snap in half. Both ends of the ship collapsed on each other. What was left of the yacht began sinking fast.

Kayden lost his footing and was thrown forward towards the center of the ship. In a second, he could see water rushing upwards from the center of the lounge. Both women were thrown to the ground and rolled towards the crack.

With his remaining strength, he fought gravity using what structural elements he could grab on to. If he stayed there, eventually he would be sucked down in between the two flooding sections of the ship with no place left to go except into the depths of the sea. Instead, he made his escape toward the closest side of the ship.

Rather than fight for their lives, the women put everything they had into their screams. They clung on to protruding pipes and structure. Before diving off into the water, Kayden looked back at them. For a second, he considered a rescue attempt.

There was no time. Not even a minute had passed since the total collapse, and the ship was nearly submerged. Kayden left the ship, crashing into the water twenty feet below. The satellite craft drifted only a few paddles away from his splash.

Coming up for air, Kayden looked back to see only a ten foot section still descending towards the deepest floor below. He wasted no time in the freezing water before climbing into the rubber satellite craft. By the time he made it in the boat, the yacht had disappeared. Only floating remains of the top section were visible in the distance.

Kayden breathed and allowed his heartbeat to slow. When he gathered himself to digest the last few minutes, he couldn't help but feel new. Even after considering his bruised ribs, the need for stitches in his facial wounds, and a possible concussion, his lungs felt stronger and his limbs felt tighter. There was something else mixed in with his blood. As a man of medicine, he knew it was more than just adrenaline. The unprovoked seizure he had survived had made him into something more. The world moved at his will. Anything in his way, anything that threatened him, would somehow move.

If only I could control it, Kayden thought.

When looking out into the dark, he felt a fear he hadn't approached in all his days. He had achieved the revenge he had sought. But now what? Everything would change. Nothing would be the same. He had no direction. No control.

The only thing he had in mind was to return home and find a way to put things back together. Kayden fired up the engine to the craft and steered it toward the glowing coast.

She had enough. Staying at home was no longer a comfortable choice. The Archer home was in tears, both sober and drunken. Grace could not continue her attempts to coax her mother out of her lifeless trance. Nor could she listen to the boozed rants by her father. She couldn't be the mediator in this. The sounds of college angst channeling through the dorms was, somehow, more appealing.

Yet, she sought quiet and neutrality. Her father's words from earlier in the day smothered her thoughts.

"I can't even call him my son," Richard Archer said wiping the tears from his face with the hand that wasn't holding a stiff glass of bourbon. At first, Grace considered it to be another mindless rant; one of many during the last few days.

Grace entered the hospital through the public entrance, but immediately took an off limits stairwell up to the 8th floor, just like she had since her senior year of high school. It troubled her as to why most of the light fixtures above the stairwell were broken and the dark stairwell was covered in fragments of glass.

On the 8th floor, Grace made sure the late night staff didn't see her sneaking into an unattended lab. She quickly and silently edged to the door and slid in the key her brother had made for her. Once inside, she took a deep breath and tossed her bag of books on a tabletop. She flicked on the lights and took a seat at one of the several desks in the room. The glass cabinets that surrounded her remained bare and dusty as always.

Just as she set her head down on the cold table, she heard the clinking sound of glass containers. The door to the lab next door was open. She became very alert, very quickly.

"Hello?" Grace called out.

No answer.

She got up and gently walked to the doorway. She stuck her head in to investigate.

"Hello?"

A laptop provided the only glow in the room. A microscope and other devices were connected the computer. Yet, there was no one at the driver's seat. She rounded the desk to take a look at the screen. The image was a live microscopic camera feed. Blood cells were being analyzed. Countless times, Grace had seen similar images in her brother's work.

She could hear breathing coming from the darkest corner of the room. A figure stood, hiding in the corner.

"Who is that?" Grace stepped back.

The figure didn't answer. But after a stressful moment, a man stepped into the glow.

"Kayden!" Grace took a big step toward him with arms open wide.

"Stop!" Kayden ordered sternly.

Grace froze in her steps.

"Don't get close to me," Kayden ordered.

"What's wrong?" Grace asked.

"Get back against the wall, Grace."

"Why? Kayden, what's going on?"

"Do it Grace."

She took several steps backwards and pinned herself in a corner, several feet away from Kayden. When her back hit the corner, she took a seat on the ground and squeezed her legs together.

Kayden stepped back behind the laptop and punched in commands. On the table was the vile that he had used to collect Mr. Armand's blood, before he set him on fire.

"That sick son-of-a-bitch," Kayden spoke to the machine, shaking his head.

"Who?" Grace asked.

Kayden wouldn't answer. He couldn't even begin to explain. Armand was right. He did carry a poison in his veins; a rare virus that could devour female reproductive organs so rapidly that no treatment would cage the symptoms. No cure had been developed, especially for something so rare. Yet, no harm would be done to any man that carried this virus. In fact, any routine blood test would easily overlook it.

Kayden could barely fathom how dangerous this virus was. If any female contracted this poison, she'd be dead in a month. And not an easy month; a dreadful, agonizing month ending in certain doom. Part of him wanted Armand back for a couple of reasons. He wanted to throw him in a lab and try and find a way to end this thing. But also, Kayden felt he hadn't been punished enough. *How could someone knowingly spread this around?* This was a new breed of evil he had only read about in books or seen on screens.

The worst part, it was contagious through sex. After looking at his own blood under the microscope, he found that his wife had done more than make him a raging vigilante. She had made him a carrier of this deadly virus. Any hopes of a rewarding relationship with another woman were out of the question.

"Kayden. Please talk to me."

He heard her plea, but stayed focused on his research.

"Where have you been?"

Still, Kayden offered no response.

"Mom won't speak. Dad is drinking his face off, rambling on about nothing. I can't take it anymore. We need you."

Kayden jammed into the keyboard with force.

"Are you listening to me? Kayden!"

"Yes!" Kayden growled and slammed his fist down. At the instant his hand hit the desk, a glass cylinder on the counter behind him shattered into pieces for no apparent reason.

This happened so quickly, Grace barely had time to process it.

"Yes," he said, calmer this time, "I am listening. Let's talk about something else. Please."

"Are you okay?"

Kayden looked at her as if to say, *what do you think?*

"What did you do to your face?" She could see the bandage and fresh stitches above his eye.

"Not important."

"Are you going to see mom? Please go see her, she needs you."

"I will. Soon."

"Have you spoken to Paul?"

"Not in several days."

"Are you not going to tell me where you have been?"

Grace took the refusal to answer the simple question as a *no.*

"Paul is in bad shape. His son. He is missing. Eight years old. Vanished in the middle of a school day."

Kayden stopped his flood of keyboard commands.

"What?"

"They don't have a clue. They have looked everywhere. Cops say it could be related to a massive string of disappearances. Young kids have been going missing from Philly to Roanoke. It's like someone is snatching up kids all over."

Even without electricity, the ceiling fan above Kayden started to spin. Grace found this confusing, but blew it off.

"How many kids are missing? "

"Dozens. Close to fifty."

"Jesus."

Grace got back to her feet, feeling a little braver now that there was conversation in the air.

"You would think they would have caught whoever is doing this."

Kayden shook his head. He closed his laptop and removed a portable thumb drive from the side of the machine. He discarded a few items including the vile and the specimen in the microscope.

"Can you come home? See Mom and Dad?"

"Not now."

"Why not?"

Kayden took a deep breath. He put down his things and sat back down. He couldn't ignore his only sibling any longer.

"Grace, things will be different for now on. I've...changed. I won't be going back to the usual routine. I can't explain it now, but trust me when I say that whatever happens next is for the best."

"I don't understand."

"And neither do I. And I need you to hold things together at home so that I can figure this out."

"I need you, Kayden."

"Grace. All that I used to know about reality is gone. All the rules, limitations. They simply do not exist. I wish I could explain. I do. But I can't."

"Is it about Cindy? Do you think you might know what happened to her?"

Kayden didn't answer. He shoved the instruments back in their storage areas and prepared to depart the lab.

"Where are you going?" Grace yelled, finally losing her temper.

All four of the lab tables slid against the floor, a few feet away from Kayden.

"What difference does it make?" he growled through clenched teeth.

Grace looked around the room, trying to understand why the tables had suddenly shifted. There was no possible answer. She became overwhelmed with terror and fled the room. She left her bag in the lab and blasted through the doors and down the stairwell, the glass of the broken fixtures crushed into even smaller fragments under her feet.

Kayden wanted to stop her. He wanted to hug his kid sister and tell her everything was going to be okay. His wife's killers were brought to justice. He could move on with his life. He could find peace.

But he couldn't. Not now. He had started something new. And the only way out, was through.

As he passed through the next room and out of the lab, the lighting fixtures hanging on the ceiling smashed into pieces. Their glass fragments scattered across the floor.

MOLOCH

PHILADELPHIA

Paul Dansin had lived his life by strict Christian values. Faithful to his wife, never committed a crime worth mentioning, and he provided support to his community at every opportunity. When he could get away from the hospital, he would provide low-cost health care door-to-door for families less fortunate. His church knew him as their in-house doctor that they could easily approach with questions or concerns related to health.

The community jumped out of their homes once word spread of the disappearance of Mark Dansin. Friends, family, and members of the church all joined in the search and to support the Dansin family. Every corner of the neighborhood was scoured in hopes of finding the eight-year-old boy. The police had very little to offer but a series of questions.

"Your son, has he ever wandered off in public areas before?"

The uniformed officer held a clipboard, jamming his pen onto the pad as he questioned Paul and his wife, Julia, in their home.

Paul's head hung low like a broken man who had begun to lose hope. He pulled at what was left of his hair. His wife worked to comfort him.

"Nothing out of the ordinary. He's a little boy. They do that." Paul answered, his mind scattered.

"When was the last time you remember him wandering off in public?"

Paul exploded out of his seat. "Are you serious? Is that how you are going to find my son? If that's the case, I shouldn't be here. I need to be out there, looking for him!"

"Paul?" his wife called.

He had already thrown on his coat and grabbed his keys before his wife began to question his intentions.

"I'm sorry. I have to go. I have to try."

"Paul wait!" Julia yelled.

Paul pulled open the front door and pushed through the screen door. He only took a step before someone obstructed his path.

The man before him was barely familiar; tired, cut, and bruised. His clothes smelled of fire and smoke, and his usual clean-cut appearance was camouflaged.

"Kayden!" Paul's anguish seemed to escape for a brief moment and was replaced by surprise.

"How can I help?"

Paul reached out and embraced Kayden and held him tightly. Kayden could feel the pain enveloping Paul.

"What can I do, old friend?"

"Can you take me to the church?" Paul whispered to Kayden.

"Of course."

Strangely, leaving Julia on the front porch to deal with the police seemed to be more difficult for Kayden than it was for Paul. During the short and familiar drive to the St. Matthew's Parish, what was left of Paul's spirit fell apart. Never had Kayden witnessed such non-physical agony.

Kayden pulled Paul into the unlocked doors of the church and plopped him down in a pew. They were greeted by the familiar face of Father Randel, who had been with the church long enough to have baptized Kayden when he was a few weeks old. Father Randel sat down close and immediately began to bring the pieces of Paul Dansin back together with prayer.

Having trouble finding comfort with the two men in prayer, Kayden took a stroll down the aisle towards the altar. St.

Matthew's tall ceilings were carved with the typical sculptures of the biblical cast, and in the middle behind the altar stood a statue of the crucifixion of Jesus Christ. The sight of the altar brought him back to his wife's funeral. A day of ritual seemed like a waste of time and energy. How destroyed he was on that dark day of mourning, he thought. The woman he had thought to be his soul mate had vanished forever. Yet in all actuality, their marriage ended up being a temporary escape from loneliness.

She was never a part of him. It all seemed like the perfect coupling, when it was merely an illusion. Perhaps, this was his sacrifice. Like Christ, he was to endure suffering so the rest of man can be relieved of their suffering. The power he was gradually learning to control had been a gift. Much like Christ's abilities, this gift made him more than man. Was he the new savior, he questioned his existance as he stared into the cross.

A white-robed clergyman appeared from a doorway in the corner of the chapel carrying a satchel. He wore thin, silver glasses which stood out over his dark skin. The clergyman and Kayden met eyes. Kayden remembered his name, Deacon Gregory James. He only assisted Father Randal, and never spoke during service. He taught Sunday school and was known to spend his time researching Christianity, as well as other faiths of the world.

Deacon James did not stay and chat. Even in the late hours of the night, he seemed to have an agenda. The Deacon wouldn't take the time to say hello to either Kayden or Paul. He darted out of the room in a hurry.

Kayden remained transfixed on the statue of Christ and the nails in his hands and feet. Kayden had never been a man of considerable faith. He had been much like the common Christian; calling himself a Christian without any study of the Bible, attending church when it was convenient, saying the blessing before a family dinner. He considered his mother to carry the weight of the family faith. So, the supernatural had never been an interest of his. But as he relived the events of the previous days while staring at the cross, his feelings toward the supernatural had reversed.

"How are you?" Father Randel said from behind.

Kayden turned. The preacher had left Paul to his prayers to join Kayden. His hands folded in front of his slightly bulging stomach.

"Sorry?" Kayden replied.

"How are you dealing with your loss?"

In a flash, Kayden rewound his thoughts to the murders, the robberies, and the destruction of the yacht.

"The best way that I can."

Father Randel nodded. "You made us all proud. The church, the community, your family, your mother. She was exhausted with her worries, when you were born…"

Father Randel reseated his glasses on his wrinkled nose and fixed his white collar.

"When I was born?" Kayden prompted the clergyman to explain.

"Let me show you something."

Father Randel led Kayden to his office, which consisted of only a bare desk, an entertainment center with no television or stereo, and a fish tank with no fish. It did contain a massive wardrobe, which the priest opened and fetched out a cloth. He handed the thick, white cloth to Kayden.

Kayden looked at the fabric and immediately noticed burn marks in the form of reddish discolorations and a smoother texture.

"Did you use this to put out a fire?" Kayden asked.

"No. I used this to baptize you."

Kayden didn't understand. The smile on the Father's face implied that he was merely jesting, but the outlandish explanation would only allow for speculation. Kayden cocked his head, signaling his confusion.

"You drove your mother mad from the day you were born until the second you were baptized. Your father thought she was having a mental breakdown, but she was persistent. I, myself, did not...could not believe the stories she described."

Kayden took a seat on an old, swivel desk chair.

"She swore that during your time alone, she would experience what must have been hallucinations. Objects dancing around the nursery. Temperatures rising to unbearable levels. Visions of an indescribable nature."

Father Randel gently took the cloth from Kayden and placed it back in his wardrobe.

"No one believed her. She was the only one that experienced these strange occurrences. They placed her in a hospital, assuming she was ill and needed attention. I shall never doubt your mother's words again. When you arrived at my altar, I..."

The Father stuttered, trying to find the correct words to effectively explain. Kayden leaned forward in his chair. His attention was sold.

"You wouldn't believe me if I tried to explain to you what I endured, what my mind endured. But there is no hiding from the truth. When I held you in that cloth, you felt as if you were boiling in my very arms. I didn't even bother with the rinse cup. I dipped you in so quickly, I might as well have dropped you in the holy water."

A day ago, Kayden would have found his way out of the room and away from this outlandish jabbering. But after his recent experiences at sea, he was much more permissive.

"When I pulled you out, my mind came back to me and your infant skin felt almost frigid. That ended your mother's so-called delusions. After that day, she spoke of nothing but wonderful times with her son. It's as if you were washed away of...whatever might have been..."

The priest took a minute to formulate his phrase, before letting his emotions carry his words.

"The Lord has a gift for each of us. A different gift for every open hand. "

Kayden stood up and paced around the office, staring at

the bland design of the rug. Possibilities stormed through his mind.

"No one but Deacon James will give me the time of day with that story. Oh, I am sure there is an explanation that makes perfect sense, something that I am just overlooking." The priest put away the cloth. "You must excuse Deacon James and his rude behavior. Once he gets in high gear, you couldn't stop him for the second coming."

Kayden blew the priest's apology off. Only one word rang in his mind: gift.

"Don't think on this too much, my son. I only wish to give your mind something else to chew on, if only briefly. I couldn't begin to imagine what a loss like yours will do to a man's soul."

Kayden thanked the preacher for his time and excused himself. He gathered up enough pieces of Paul to get him back home and to his living room couch, where Paul insisted he remain until he had answers to his questions.

Julia let her husband sit peacefully and brought Kayden to the side. She privately told Kayden about a visitor that had arrived while Paul and Kayden had spent the last hour at the church. An odd character who offered his services in helping to find their son in exchange for whatever information they had received about the progress of the investigation. The man introduced himself only by the name Bain. Julia described this Bain character as genuinely interested in helping, but his aggressive tone and spastic mannerisms made her nervous; too nervous to allow the conversation to continue. "I am close. So very close to catching this fiend. If you want your son back, you are going to have to act quickly" were the last words Julia allowed Bain to offer.

Bain left his number written on a gas receipt. His words suggested that the disappearance of Mark Dansin was somehow related to a person Bain sought for his own reasons. While Julia was quick to dismiss the intense visitor, the incident seized Kayden's complete attention. Kayden recommended, with good-minded deceit, that she not mention this to the police and let Kayden take care of this Bain character.

Kayden left the Dansin household emotionally exhausted and physically beaten down. He knew what direction he was going, but he would need rest to rationally find the next step. He needed sleep, and he knew exactly where he could find it: the place where he grew into a man. Kayden went home.

It wasn't the first time he had been woken up on the porch by his mother. In the time of his youth, Kayden had thought he was the only one in the family that knew he snuck out of the house on a regular basis. When the snow fell so vastly that no one could hear Kayden's feet hit the lawn, he raced around the neighborhood and the nearby woods with his gang of friends until the sun came up. He would wander by himself if his friends didn't have the guts to join him. He had ten times the energy his friends from school had. A night of building sled tracks to race down in the dark or throwing eggs at cars in the middle of the night was not tiring for young Kayden.

His mother, Alice Archer, experienced a thrill the instant she looked out her living room window and onto her covered porch. She was shocked to see a grown man asleep on patio furniture, and filled with warmth to see her only son, regardless of his odd visit. Just as she had done in his teenage years, she nudged him until he awoke, then walked his sleep depraved body to the nearest bed inside and let him get a few more hours of comfortable sleep.

Kayden rested in his old room, which had been transformed into a guest room, for the remainder of the morning and most of the afternoon. Alice couldn't pry herself from Kayden's cracked bedroom door. Every few minutes, she could peak in to the room and watch her only son sleep.

She had a hot meal in front of him the very minute Kayden awoke and had finished washing the filth off of his body. He couldn't remember the last time he ate, as if he had been living on anger and adrenaline. Richard and Alice didn't seem to know how to start a conversation as they watched their son refuel. The three of them hadn't spoken to one another much at all since Cindy's death. The air between them was thick enough to taste.

"Had an interesting conversation with Father Randel. He told me a story about the time when I was born, a story that I had never heard before." Kayden said, attempting to start a conversation.

Alice lifted her head, the braid of silky grey hair rested on her chest. The expression on her thin face turned from a neutral, patient smile to a look of crushing embarrassment.

"God Damn it!" Richard pounded his fist into the kitchen table and stood up. He looked for something to punch, throw, or kick. He then stopped himself and laced his fingers behind his head, as if to surrender.

This was not the reaction Kayden was prepared for. If anything, he was trying his hand at small talk with his parents. He had no intention of provoking this amount of emotion, nor did he think it was necessary to get riled up about a superstitious tale of hallucinations and babies hot enough to burn cloth. Looking into his mother's eyes, he knew that he had pulled out the dust from under the rug.

"That son-of-a-bitch should have kept his damn mouth shut. It wasn't his place to tell him. We would have," Richard Archer barked at his wife. He then paused and folded his arms, leaning against the sink.

Tears rolled from Alice's face. She reached out and held her sons hand.

"We thought it best that you didn't know. Nothing good would have come from it."

Kayden nodded, still baffled by their reaction.

"Your father loves you like his very own. He has been there since the very beginning. He is your father, anyway you look at it." Alice said, eagerly trying to convince.

"We are thankful that we brought you into this world. I

wouldn't have it any other way, no matter how it happened. The damned doctors, our friends, our family even, they told us not to keep you," Richard added.

Kayden was far beyond confused.

"I know now, as crazy as it may appear, that you were meant to happen. God gave me a son. I am forever blessed. We are forever blessed," said Alice.

"Mother? What are you talking about? Father Randel told me about the hallucinations, the strange things that happened during my first days alive, how I somehow burned his cloth at my baptism. So, what are YOU talking about?"

Alice leaned back and looked to her husband. Richard dropped his chin to his chest and sighed.

"Never mind dear, just a misunderstanding. Can I get you anything else?"

"No, we are talking about this." Kayden demanded.

"Forget about it, Kay. I'll be in the garage," Richard began his retreat. Alice quickly jumped from her chair, taking dishes to the sink.

Kayden's drinking glass shattered against the kitchen floor as he exploded out of his chair. Richard and Alice assumed that Kayden did so by throwing the glass with his hands. They were wrong in that assumption.

"No! I've had enough lies. Can someone please give me a little honesty?"

Richard Archer always kept the wooden back door open and the screen door shut to let the air circulate, which allowed another pair of ears to absorb the conversation in the kitchen. Grace kept herself hidden against the brick wall in the shadows of the back patio. She heard every word. The conversation that followed Kayden's uproar and request for truth was a devastating blow to Grace; so crushing that she could not bring herself to enter the Archer home.

It was much like a stab to the heart to hear that her brother was not born from both Richard and Alice Archer. The conversation she had overheard revealed the painful truth that

Richard was not Kayden's biological father. From what Grace had heard, nine months before Kayden was born, Alice Archer was raped during a Peace Corps mission in South America and became pregnant. Regardless of the opposing suggestions she received from all sides, Alice gave birth to Kayden.

Her family was everything to her. She absorbed every sound, every morsel of affection. It was her fuel. Unlike most teenagers growing up a chaotic era, rebelliousness was never a quality she indulged with. She wasn't the perfect child. She made mistakes; she stayed out late on occasion. She experimented to a degree. Passed on by her father Richard, she was able to take that determined and confident step forward and not hesitate. Richard always stressed that you miss all the shots you don't take. Both Alice and Kayden objected to that behavior. They were both more conservative and methodical. They rarely took a step forward before thoroughly examining the pros and cons. What wild, rambunctious characteristics she maintained she also shared with her father, who never missed a chance to enjoy himself.

Alice was far more sheltered and inhibited. She lived her life not for herself, but for her children and for the world. Ever since her youth, Alice had been involved in peace rallies, donation drives, and any and all causes for humanity. Without question, she was a woman of unmatched faith in Christ. The Church was her inspiration. The Bible was her fuel. Alice had trouble relating to her two children, who were growing up in a far different era then she had matured in. Grace was very accepting of the Christian faith, while Kayden couldn't be bothered by the word of the Lord. He was far more interested in the studies and accomplishments of man.

During that horrid family conversation, Richard Archer grew so emotional that he darted out of the house and took off in his pickup. The whispers between Alice and Kayden afterwards were too faint for Grace to digest. Grace covered her face so as to not expose herself as an eavesdropper as she broke down in painful tears on her back porch. Much of her wished she hadn't been so inquisitive that evening.

"Because it is innocence that will deliver us from evil. It is innocence that will fuel the chariot which carries us to His kingdom. We must cherish innocence. Nurture innocence. Worship innocence. Conserve innocence. Pay no mind to the cost. For once we triumph over the opposition, there will be no need to rebuild, restock, maintain, or progress. We will forever be in the light of God."

The scant audience that sat in the pews before Lance Woodard provided no reaction whatsoever, much less their full attention. There was no honorific title preceding his name, like most of the men who spoke from the Bible or preached their interpretation. Yet, he wore the approachable uniform of a clergyman with a clerical collar behind a black dress shirt, tucked into black slacks. Rumor told that throughout Lance's life, he had sought to become a priest but had never been accepted by an established congregation. The dozen attendees that were spread out through the converted Philadelphia grade-school theater hall may have only been there to hide.

"Trust the youth to show us the way. Their unmarred souls are the only ones that can see through the dark. When the wave of the damned and the black caps of sin wash upon our shores, it is the youth that will show no fear. And one without fear cannot be harmed by the tides of hell. It is innocence that will crush the opposition."

Those that had known Lance Woodard from the whispers and the occasional hate-blog may have known of his extremist stance on Christian faith. He had been known to show up at political rallies with a megaphone, broadcasting his thoughts in a usually unsuccessful attempt to convert the subject matter to his ideology. He spoke out against ministers and priests known to be more accepting of the whole community and other faiths and lifestyles. Lance did not carry many followers and remained much of a lone solider, fighting the 'good fight' in his own way.

Lance had let his usual short haircut grow out on top and curl. His hair bounced from side to side as he jumped into his red Chevy Bronco shortly after his thirty minutes expired at the lecture hall. He left, appalled by the fact that he was the only speaker of the evening that was not allowed the full hour. During the drive, he blasted loud, aggressive rants from his stereo. The ranting was actually his voice being played back from a recording. His mind was barely conscious of the road as he drove through the Pennsylvania countryside; he studied his own unique theological aberration instead.

Far away from the streets of Philadelphia, the drive ended off-road and deep in the woods, although the journey did not end as the truck's engine was silenced. Lance traded his glossy dress shoes for hiking boots. He continued on foot with a pack on his back. There was no trail for him to follow, yet he passed through the untamed woods without hesitation or concern for navigation, marching on with a proud smile.

Twenty minutes of steady advancement through the brush took him miles away from any other members of mankind. Once Lance reached his destination, he let out a sigh of relief and let his pack fall off of his shoulders. After catching his breath, he allowed his legs to buckle, landing on his knees with a thud.

Before his genuflection were two open graves. He kneeled before these two holes, each of which was too big for small animals and too small for an adult human. Two mounds of freshly shoveled dirt sat to the sides of each grave.

"The power, which once flourished within you, has been stripped from your holy grasp by the ones who you have blessed. You gave them a chance for eternal joy, and they have repaid you with tyranny. They have declared you as false. Devoted their love to themselves, their lies, and their betrayals. Those that claim to love you, beg you to ease their pain and frustrations. How dare they?"

A body lay in each grave wrapped tightly in white cloth; the flesh of two children, inert with their hands crossed over their chests. Lance rose and retrieved two silver cylinders from his pack. He carried them in a white fabric, much like a priest sharing the Body of Christ with his followers.

"I dare not beg of you. My every breath is an offer of my gratitude to you alone. I sweat, only to give back to you, to help you regain your strength so that you may take back this world from the plague of sin that feasts on your creation."

Lance poured a rusty liquid from the cylinders onto each of the bodies below.

"Soon, my lord, you will have the army that you will need to control this world again. Allow me to help you. Take these souls. They have not yet been corroded by the evil that stands against you. They are pure. They will serve you well, my Lord."

With a lit match for each grave, Lance ignited the white fabric covering the bodies. The flames soared high and mighty within seconds. Lance breathed in the fumes deeply into his lungs.

"Hear them Lord. Hear their cries. They call only for you."

In the windy turmoil of the violent flames, a wailing cry rang from one of the graves, then another from the next grave. Cries of severe pain of the still breathing bodies could faintly be heard over the flames. Cries of children dying from the fire that engulfed their bodies.

Hear them, Lord!"

She ran. Rather than stop to get in her car parked only a few strides away, Grace ran. The young woman was both horrified and devastated to the point that she could not gather a rational thought.

Perhaps running was her instinct, for Grace had run the same route as a growing child; same sidewalk, same start, same finish. If she had been frightened by a monster on the television or fearful of the arguments between her mother and father, she would run to the place that would nurture her, calm her down and make everything feel safe again. Church—it was her haven, and had been for many years. Only a few blocks away stood St. Matthew's Parish.

Never had she run from a conversation with her brother. However, the early morning conversation with Kayden was like no other she had with him, or anyone else for that matter. After spending a considerable amount of time the night before eavesdropping from outside her home, she felt compelled to confess her encroachment.

When she came home, Kayden was awake and exhausted. His face was unshaven and his eyes begged for sleep. Grace found him sitting on the sofa, elbows resting on his knees, staring at the floor. He did not react to her entrance in the slightest way. Grace's first words were an apology for her intrusiveness. She wanted him to know that she had listened to the conversation he had last night with their parents. Kayden had no response.

Grace then asked for an explanation of the freakish evening at the hospital. Again, he did not respond. She asked when he would return to work, trying desperately to draw any signs of life from her only sibling. Nothing.

She asked about Paul Dansin, and if they had found his son. The moment she asked, she felt her body start to perspire. An odd warm breeze seemed to push around the living room, gently tossing the curtains and the plants hanging in the corners. She found this strange, but was more focused on provoking conversation. Still, Kayden said nothing and kept his eyes on the ground. Grace withdrew to the kitchen for a coffee mug of water for her brother. Part of her wanted to leave, to let him deal with this new development in peace, yet her compassion drove her to provide support.

She stuck the cup up to his face, insisting that he take a drink. He did not. Instead, he spoke.

"I killed him."

Grace almost dropped the mug.

"What?" she asked.

"I killed them all."

"Who?"

"I found the one who took Cindy, and I killed him. And everyone with him."

"Kayden?"

"They are gone. And I am here."

"This is not good. This is really not good, Kay," she started to tremble and took a step away.

He looked up at her. "And why is that?"

"Because you can't just do that. They are probably looking for you and when they find you, they'll put you away. It's not your place."

"Not my place? Really? Then whose place is it, Grace?"

"The police. They catch people. They decide what happens. They have the power."

"Power? They have no idea what power is."

Kayden took one hard look at the coffee mug Grace held with her fingertips. Without a sound, the ceramic mug shattered into dozens of pieces and fell to the carpet. Grace, unharmed yet stunned, dropped the handle of the mug and backed against the wall.

Kayden stood, staring into her eyes.

"This life I have been living, it's pointless. And it was never meant to be like this. I was never meant to have a normal life. There has always been something more. I've always felt it." Kayden shook his head slightly. "Just know that I love you more than you could ever know, Grace. You are the only one I can trust, now. "

When Kayden stood up and stepped toward Grace, perhaps to reach in for a brotherly hug, she freaked and bolted from her home to a place she could count on for safety.

Deacon Gregory James was swiftly making his way to his office when he noticed a young woman in the pew closest to the altar. Her head rocked back and forth as she wept. The Deacon quickened his step to the back hallway of offices. He yelled to through the dark, unoccupied hall.

"Father Randal? Father Randal? There is a young lady in the house. Father Randal?"

There was no reply. It quickly became apparent that the Deacon was the only staff member in the building. He put down his satchel and shoved himself through a bathroom door. At the sink, Gregory turned on the hot water and checked himself out in the mirror.

"Slow. Slow," the Deacon whispered to himself.

Taking deep breaths, he set his glasses on the sink and washed his face with the warm water. The drops trickled off his dark skin. He pushed back the couple inches of his graying hair, only to try and smooth out the rough, uneven spots. Before he left the restroom, he took a deep breath.

Deacon James took tiny steps toward sobbing Grace. He continued to look around the room, silently praying for Father Randal to show up and relieve him. When Gregory came to within a few paces of Grace, he forced himself to speak to the troubled young woman.

"Miss?"

He whispered so softly that Grace could not hear.

"Miss?" he tried again.

Grace raised her head and looked at Deacon James.

"Can I help you?"

"I'm sorry. I didn't know where else to go," said Grace.

"Father Randal will be here any moment."

Gregory could hear the fear in her sob. He sat down at the pew about six feet away from Grace.

"Miss, why are you so troubled? Why are you here? Why are you alone?"

She sucked back her tears for a moment to speak.

"I don't know if I am going crazy or the world is crazy. Everything I have grown up to believe has been a lie. I don't know what to do."

Deacon James had always been the black sheep of the clergy. Unlike many in his field, he sought answers and never pretended to act as if he had any sound advice to give, for, in his eyes, this world was vastly unpredictable with far less structure than people are led to believe. Only when he was pressured would he play the role and shut his mouth. But the truth was Deacon James yearned for knowledge, yearned for worthwhile conversation, yearned to know all that was being hidden from him.

"The world is...crazy. There is no controlling mankind, as much as we would like to believe there is," Deacon James stuttered.

Grace looked to him as if his words began to cut into her fear.

"Things are happening that are not supposed to happen. Good people, wonderful people seem to be changing into something terrible," she continued.

"The influence..." the Deacon took his time to wrangle his words, "of good is equally matched by the influence of the enemy. We all know this to be true, but we don't want to accept that."

"I think I am starting to," Grace said, and the fear inside her showed itself clearly.

"Please, tell me why," Deacon James asked and scooted closer to her.

Grace dove right into her predicament by describing the death of her sister-in-law. She began the story all the way back from when Cindy and Kayden were married and on to her death.

She spoke of her brother, Kayden, describing him as a hero, a giver. Stubborn at times, yet he offered nothing but compassion and warmth. A passion swelled inside Kayden at a level she had never witnessed elsewhere. She idolized him. As much as he tried to convince her to try another path, she wanted to follow her heroic brother.

And then she spoke of her parents, and what she had learned the night before.

"And his birth father is...?" Gregory asked.

"I don't know. I'm not sure if anyone knows. My mother's

attackers, she called them monsters. Probably some drugged-out, pathetic rapists. They were never caught."

"And they hadn't told your brother until now?"

"Yes. It must be a terrible thing to have to accept."

"Unfathomable."

Deacon James sat back in the pew, collecting what she described. He could have shed his own tears, but he remained strong.

"Deacon James?"

"Yes, Grace?"

"If someone you loved did something criminal, something horrible, something that could get them locked away forever, would you tell someone? Would you go to the police?"

Gregory paused before answering.

"In my younger years, I would have said no. I would have told you that I could fix it myself. I could make it better."

"And now?"

"I don't know. As much as we are supposed to believe that the police are here to help, it is sometimes hard to know who to trust."

Grace did not expect this answer from a clergyman.

"Not many people, especially not those of the clergy, share my views on the world. I believe our God to be powerful beyond our imagination. I know him as my savior, my guide, and worthy of my life. But I also believe in his foe."

Grace bowed her head as if she felt it to be improper discussing such things in church.

"I know the power of God is equally matched by evil. By the laws of God, the two are allowed to influence the Earth equally. For all the many wonderful, miraculous things that are witnessed every day, there are just as many souls that become corrupted. Evil, that you could never imagine, is put into action continuously. And the only true way to stop it is inside each and every one of us. Sometimes, we need time alone, locked away, so that we can fight it off within."

Grace let her head hang low. She let the tears roll off her cheeks.

"Maybe I am just seeing things. But something is so strange about him now. I think I am losing my mind," she said.

Gregory scooted over to Grace's side and offered a gentle hand on her shoulder.

"It's like my brother has this...power now. He can smash things by just looking at them. Move things around the room without touching them."

Deacon James took his hand away and leaned back. His mouth dropped slightly. He breathed in deeply, almost gasping.

"What...What? What did he do?"

"Sorry?"

Awkwardly, the Deacon stared at her. She knew his mind was spinning at full speed.

"What did your brother do that would make you want to tell the police?"

She looked at him, signaling her vulnerability. He saw right into her. She had to give in. The only way out was through.

"He killed them. Whoever it was that took Cindy's life. He killed him. And everyone involved."

Gregory's eyes filled with tears. His hands began to shake. He became very fidgety.

"And now. He's a different person. He's like...he's like a monster," she added.

The Deacon folded his hands, trying to keep them from shaking. He grew enormously nervous. He could not even sit still. He went to his feet.

Flooded in guilt, Grace knew instantly that she had made a mistake by opening her trap and telling the preacher man of her brother's crime. She only wished she had a friend that she could trust with the information who could help her process. But she didn't. The Deacon just happened to be a set of ears close by as she ventilated. She felt eager to beg The Deacon for secrecy, but the anxiety rushing the sweat from her pours made it far too difficult to remain still.

"Thank you for listening to me. I hope that you will let me handle this on my own and let me help my brother. I can assure you, I will do what is right."

She rose and wiped away her tears, ready to make her exit and face the challenge ahead.

"Thank you for your words. You seem very...kind," she added, trying to smooth him over with whatever compliments came to mind.

She began to march down the aisle.

"Wait, please. Wait," the Deacon requested. She stopped and turned. Deacon James stood there shaking, which frightened Grace. "The man that killed...Cee...Cee..."

"Cindy?" Grace offered.

"Yes! Cindy. Was he...was he..." the Deacon could hardly pull a sentence together.

"Are you okay?" she felt as if he was on the verge of having a breakdown.

"Was the man he killed her lover?"

Grace's teary, painful face seemed to dry up and almost crack. Frozen by the Deacon's question, she couldn't answer with her voice. She nodded.

If Grace had stuck around to see Gregory's reaction, she might have called an ambulance. The man nearly went into shock. As Grace hurried out of the church doors, Gregory kneeled at the altar, shaking madly. From his mouth he mumbled a prayer; an unintelligible plea for help from his God. Grace's anxiety and the concern for her brother's current state seemed juvenile compared to the horror that the Deacon was poisoned by.

Grace was met by Father Randal on her exit. She shared only a cordial acknowledgement with the priest before quickly leaving the area. Father Randal trotted to his friend, who was obviously in some sort of panic. He reached out from behind Deacon James to get a comforting hold on his friend and coworker. The instant Father Randal's hands touched him, the Deacon screamed.

Father Randal jumped back.

"Gregory? What is it?"

He appeared not to hear the question and continued mumbling his frantic prayer.

For close to three hours, Bain Whelan sat in the driver's seat of his blacked-out SUV, listening to the news on the radio. Gradually becoming impatient, he scratched at his head of closely trimmed red hair and rubbed his arms that were covered British and Christian tattoos. The rest of his tattoos were under his white t-shirt and grey work slacks.

On the dash was a picture of a freckled little girl with red pigtails. As anyone could have guessed by their similarities, the little girl was Bain's daughter, who he hadn't seen in over a year. She had disappeared one afternoon while enjoying a comfortable day in the park with friends. Not a day went by that Bain did not devote to finding his daughter again.

From the stereo, a female's voice reported, "...activists have not uncovered any answers to the strange and massive disappearances of over six-hundred villagers. This marks the third occurrence in less than a year of what appears to be a complete dissipation of an entire tribe in this particular South American region. Some speculate political genocide. This year, CoNam, a global textile manufacturer, is building a multi-million dollar factory right on top of the village of Tupan, a tribal area in the Pampas Grassland that once was a home to over three thousand villagers who have also mysteriously vanished. No known investigation is underway."

The radio spat out another sour turn of events on the public news station. Bain shook his head. His phone vibrated on his middle console. He received a text message: *He's wrapping up.*

Bain grabbed the photo of the little girl on the dash and exited the vehicle. He walked along the city sidewalk towards a small library.

Inside a small meeting room of the library, Lance Goodard preached to a small and mostly uninterested house. The theme of his message: One Nation *For* God, Not Under. It was a political ideal that outlined a new form of government strictly adhering to the Bible and transforming the Constitution to look more like the Ten Commandments. Few listened in. However, there were three attendees who seemed to be tremendously focused on every word Lance uttered. Each of the three seemed slightly disagreeable.

One of them was a young, athletic-looking woman in her early thirties, with her brown hair tied back, a pair of tight black jeans, and a loose-fitting white sweatshirt. Aside from occasional glances at her cell phone, she stared at Lance as he ranted. A few seats back, a beast of a man wearing all black with dark, square sunglasses, sat with his legs stretched wide. His head was completely shaved, allowing his dark-skinned head to shine underneath the fluorescent light. He chewed his gum boldly. On the other side of the room, a baby-faced college kid sat jittering as if it was cold, holding his knee and appearing anxious. He could not keep still. At one point, he threw his stained hoodie over his head. None of the three seemed to belong in such a place, listening to a lecture of religious context.

Lance never hung around after his speeches to answer any questions. When attendees were able to speak to him, maybe even offer an opposing view, Lance would shrug it off as if his word could not be questioned. The young lady, the giant man behind the shades, and the college kid left only seconds after Lance departed. Outside the library, Bain Whelan awaited.

"Lance Goodard, right?" Bain stepped in front of Lance's quick stride.

Lance, irritated by this unknown man obstructing his progress, did not even motion a response.

"You are Lance Goodard. I know, I have heard you speak in front of many. Say, you show a lot of brass up there, speaking the good Lord's word. "

Lance obviously took this as a compliment and stopped to entertain Bain.

"Thank you, friend. And your name?"

"Bain. Bain Whelan."

They shook hands. Bain smiled wildly.

"You've just finished another lecture, have ya?" Bain asked.

"Yes. Another night of service to the Lord."

"It's a bloody shame I missed that."

"Don't you worry friend. There will be more."

"Aye. Dare I ask you for a favor, preacher?"

"You certainly may."

"A prayer for my daughter," Bain handed Lance the photo that was stuck in the dash of the parked SUV. The same SUV the three interesting attendees climbed into together while Bain and Lance spoke.

Lance's face reset.

"She's been missing for months now. We don't have a clue where the little lamb has gotten off to. Sweetest angel on the planet," Bain explained.

The photo shook in Lance's grasp. He stared into the eyes of the little girl in the photo, as if he was reliving memory.

"Mr. Goodard?"

No response. He seemed to have drifted off.

"Mate?"

"Yes, yes. Sure. I shall pray for her. I am sure she..."

"Sir?"

"I am sure she is somewhere safe."

"I do hope so."

"Good day to you."

"And you, Mr. Goodard."

Bain offered a handshake to Lance, which was accepted. Yet Bain did not stop with just a handshake. Instead, Bain pulled in Lance for a quick and kindhearted, almost forceful, embrace.

With the sun urging to set on the city street, Bain jumped into the SUV. Sitting in the vehicle were the three spectators from the library—Cari Love, Gar Sworn, and Alton Harper.

The striking Cari Love, the hard-edged brunette, sat in the front passenger seat holding a crudely shaped blade against her leg. It took her two gruesome marriages before Cari wised up

_PAD

and began to defend herself from the fists of men. Once a timid, gentle lady, she trained to become a fearsome woman. Her last husband would spend the rest of his life without his manhood, which she deprived him of with the slash of a blade. Settling that score had satisfied an appetite and gave her new life with a new direction. After one conversation with Bain, Cari Love volunteered her assistance to his campaign.

Gar Sworn sat in the far back of the SUV and had not taken off his sunglasses. Spending months under the sun near the equator, crawling inch by inch, fighting communism, Gar Sworn had enough of the sunlight or any light at that matter, and rarely showed his eyes. The veteran left fighting for what he saw as a political agenda, to fighting for his own agenda. He was well versed in gunpowder, and he used it well and often.

As usual, Alton Harper was glued to a laptop screen. He had spent most of his short life in screens, jamming away at the loopholes and short cuts of databases. He held bitterness toward the world, probably due to all the dodgy info he had come across in his explorations. Acting on his bitterness, he had destroyed numerous electronic infrastructures, one off-shore account at a time.

"You see him, Al?"

"I got him. Next time just stick the bug on him. You don't have to put it in his pocket."

"Do you have the man, or not?"

"I got him. Relax," Alton replied.

"This all ends tonight. Is that crystal?" Bain asked the group.

"Goddamn right," Gar added.

Bain brought the vehicle to life and sped down the city street while Alton navigated. Bain had dropped a tracking device on Lance Goodard's person, which allowed Alton to monitor his location. They kept a vigilant distance from Lance's red Chevy Bronco as it raced out of the city.

Before long, buildings along the side of the road were replaced by trees. Alton's signal on Lance became more and more disrupted the further they were from the city. Bain made sure to trail Lance's vehicle by several car lengths, but kept him in sight.

Lance broke off of the main road and charged forward onto an unpaved road that seemed to lead deep into the brush. Bain pulled the truck over on the main stretch of highway, and uncomfortably let Alton's laptop be their eyes, for following Lance into the woods would most likely give away their pursuit. Alton's machine told the gang that Lance had broken off the paved road and was maneuvering slowly on some unknown path.

Bain made the executive decision to ditch the truck and follow on foot. From the back hatch, Gar retrieved an all black, double barrel, 12-gauge shotgun. It matched his appearance faultlessly. He handed Cari a pistol and what looked like a customized jagged hatchet, which stretched from hip to foot. She hadn't said a word for the entire ride, or even held much of an expression. But when she took the blade from Gar, she seemed to light up like someone with purpose. She shoved the pistol in the back of her pants and followed Bain and Alton. Alton held the laptop in front of him like a map, as Bain shoved him along.

The four of them ran into thick brush quickly. Dead trees and fallen branches were the main obstacle. Yet with one hard swing, Cari's weapon cut through most of the wood in their path. The signal they had on Lance cut in and out, driving Bain mad. Bain cursed Alton viciously as he pushed him through the brush. Alton did his damnedest to stay focused on Lance's position and not trip over rocks and tree roots.

The sun inched down and out of the horizon as the four hunters stopped and hunched down in the rough. When they came within thirty yards of Lance's signal, they could hear both rummaging and a voice.

"What do we do now?" Alton asked their leader.

"He's stopped moving. If he has one, then he has nowhere to go. If he's there alone, we have nothing. I know this bastard won't fess up. He will take it to the grave. I don't intend on letting another child die."

They all sat silently, listening hard for the sound of a child. Hoping that they could finally catch this creep red handed and put an end to this.

"Let's get closer," Gar suggested and slowly continued on through the brush. Bain and the rest of them followed closely behind.

The group stepped lightly to avoid making any sound. Bain held a pistol down and at the ready. They approached Lance's parked Chevy Bronco and used it as cover. They could hear Lance's voice clearly, but only his voice. Bain peered over the hood of the truck.

Bain saw the back of Lance Goodard. He was praying out loud on his knees in the dirt. His hands were folded. He nodded his head up and down as he prayed. Before his knees, a deep square hole was dug into the Earth.

Rage filled Bain's veins when he saw his prey in front of an open grave. He knew what this was. He had been on this monster's trail for months now. No one had caught up to him until now, but even then, their efforts seemed to be too late.

Bain retired his secrecy and marched toward Lance. The other three followed. They approached Lance from behind and looked into the open grave. The three of them saw a body wrapped in white, small enough to be a child. Lance, unaware that he was no longer alone, continued his prayer with his eyes shut.

Gar cocked his rifle. Lance stopped his prayer when he heard the shell being loaded. He slowly turned his head to see four people staring at him. The instant he tried to cry out, Bain cuffed his mouth with his gloved hand and pulled him to his feet by his neck. Lance tried to struggle, but his efforts were pointless against Bain's grasp. Gar shoved the butt of the rifle hard into Lance's guts.

Cari did not hesitate to jump into the grave. Her face nearly exploded with tears as she hovered over the body beneath her.

She pulled the white fabric from behind the head of the body. The face of a boy appeared. What Cari had expected was a bloodless, swollen face on the verge of decomposition. Yet, the young boy's face may have been a bit bruised, but not unhealthy. She reached for his throat, checking his pulse.

"He's alive!"

Cari and Alton pulled the unconscious boy from the grave while Bain and Gar began their interrogation.

"Where are the rest of them?" Bain asked.

"You leave me be!" Lance replied, fearful.

Gar nearly kicked his head off with a shined combat boot. Blood flew from Lance's mouth along with tooth fragments. Bain bent down to get personal with Lance.

"Where are the rest of the children?"

Lance actually giggled. He pulled out a tooth that Gar had broken with his boot.

"Where are they?" Bain yelled in his face. He mashed a pistol against Lance's brow.

The young boy had a weak pulse and was barely breathing. He displayed all the signs of heavy sedation. Cari held him tightly to warm the young boy.

"Your concern for them does not fill my heart with the slightest amount of compassion. I am not fooled by servants of false Gods." Lance sneered.

Bain allowed Lance to push himself on his feet. Gar stuck the barrel of his rifle in Lance's face.

"If you truly cared for the people in this world, you would help each other, not take advantage of those who may be vulnerable," Lance stated.

"We've heard enough of your preaching," said Gar behind his rifle.

"That may be. But you haven't responded. And you surely haven't responded to God. Instead, you've turned your back on him. You've joined an enemy who offers apathetic existence and comfort, wrapped pleasantly for your indulgence. Take, take, take and take some more. Maybe you give a little of your time, maybe a little of your wealth, maybe birth children to hopelessly follow in your footsteps."

"Where is my daughter?!" Bain cried.

"Your daughter? The life that you gave to the world? Your daughter? That is a sin in itself. To bring in a new life to this world, to set it free into this world. Only to let it become like the rest of you defectors. Breeding evil is not what God has asked of you. He asks you to become part of the flock. Nurture the flock. Expand the flock."

Bain's eyes watered. He knew his heart would not be mended on that day.

"This is my crusade. My quest for God. To build his flock before the flock is plagued. Send their souls up to him, fresh, vibrant, loving, and ready to serve. It is the only way to save this world."

Tears rolled down Bain's face. He knew where Lance Goodard had sent his daughter. As much as he wanted to believe, he knew he wouldn't see her again.

"Cut this bastard down!" Bain ordered.

"My pleasure," said Gar.

Gar pointed the rifle directly at Lance's heart, only inches away. Just as he began to squeeze the trigger, the rifle was ripped from Gar's grasp and thrown far into the trees by no easily distinguishable means. No hand but Gar's had touched the gun. No serious wind had picked up. It was simply yanked away by the still air.

Gar stepped back, dazed by what had just happened. Lance's face lit up like a thousand stars. He and Gar were the only ones to witness the odd event.

"Do it already!" Bain ordered with his head turned.

"Bain?" Gar gestured.

"What?"

Bain looked to see Gar in rare form, confused and unarmed. Lance clasped his hands together and silently thanked the God above him, dropping to his knees in worship.

"What happened?" Bain asked Gar.

"The gun...it..."

"You have cold feet all the sudden? This is how it's done, my friend."

Bain lifted his pistol to Lance's dome.

As soon as the barrel touched the skin of Lance's forehead, the pistol left Bain's hands and also flew into the woods, discharging as if hit the ground several hidden yards away.

"What in God's name?" asked Bain.

A man appeared from the woods and walked into the clearing. He wore a dark trench coat and heavy, steel-toed boots. His face was unshaven. His blue eyes appeared exhausted. He marched with authority, unarmed and somehow nonthreatening. The sullen figure stopped within reasonable conversation distance of Bain. Gar had taken an extra step back, eyeing the blade Cari had set down on the grass.

"And who the fuck are you?" Bain asked.

"My name is Kayden Archer."

"Alright. And why are you here?"

"I have been following you. I've watched you hunt down this man. I've watched you catch a criminal that has slipped through the hands of the law, numerous times. I am impressed with your efforts, and disappointed with the efforts of our law."

Bain and Gar looked at each other. Both of them were baffled.

"Well, mate," Bain said, "thank you, and whatnot. But it seems that you are not the only one following us. Somebody is around here, ripping the guns from our very hands. And I don't have a fucking clue how they are do—"

Kayden cut him off. "I must apologize. That was me."

The gang of four looked at each other in disbelief.

"How?" Gar asked.

"I am not quite sure exactly."

"You are not sure. Okay nut job. Why then?" Bain asked.

"I cannot let you kill him."

"You cannot let us kill this bastard?" Bain pointed.

"He will pay for what he has done in the most painful way possible, I can promise you that. Just not here. Not now."

It was obvious that Bain wasn't going to let anyone stand in his way.

"Cari, end this crazy fuck now, please," Bain commanded.

She did not hesitate. With her pistol, she banged out round after round as she marched toward Kayden. The gun was pointed at Kayden's chest, yet Kayden did not move, did not flinch, did not even blink. He stared at Cari as she emptied her clip. She took her last shot at Kayden from point blank range, with no human way possible of missing. Yet, no lead touched Kayden. All of them heard the last shot somehow dodge Kayden and cut through the leaves above.

Everyone froze for an instant.

But Gar would not give up. He picked up Cari's blade.

"Cari!" Gar yelled and tossed the blade to Cari.

During the fraction of time when the blade was flying towards Cari, Kayden acquired his defense. He took one glance at the Bronco. The driver's side door to the truck detached from the frame and flew towards Kayden.

Cari caught the weapon and immediately swung it downward in hopes of splitting Kayden in half from the skull to his groin. Instead, her blade collided with the steel car door that Kayden used to shield himself. Kayden physically chucked the door off to the side, and Cari reared back for another strike. Before she could, her weapon left her grasp and flew into a thick tree, out of reach.

While Lance crawled into the woods on all fours, Gar came at Kayden with clinched fists. Kayden calmly dodged the haymakers Gar threw, and returned with his own fists. Unlike Gar, he did not miss.

Alton's body flew into Gar from behind. Alton's feet collided with Gar's backside, knocking Gar to the ground. Alton immediately apologized before unintentionally tripping Cari by kicking out her legs from underneath her. Alton's body was being used against his will. Kayden concentrated hard on Alton.

In what could be described as a hideous, poorly performed figure skating spin, Alton's body spun around quickly with both fists swinging around violently. Bain did not get out of the way soon enough and was nearly knocked unconscious.

Lance was upright and pushing through the woods when his feet were pulled out from underneath him. He ascended high above the tree tops, screaming wildly. His body flew over the fight and fell at nearly free fall speeds, landing in the grave he dug for the little boy.

Bain, Cari, Gar, and Alton stayed on the ground, knowing good and well they were somehow outmatched. Kayden offered a hand to Cari to assist her back on her feet. She accepted. The rest of them gradually got to their feet. The little boy, lying by a tree and still mostly wrapped up in the white cloth, began to wake up.

Kayden looked down at Lance, rolling around in pain in the grave.

"The boy's name is Mark Dansin. His family is very close to me. I can't thank you enough for finding him when you did."

Cari and Alton went to the boy, helping him sit upright.

Kayden spoke, "I want this...thing dead no less than you do. The fact that he has been able to do this for so long is unacceptable. As you might know, he's been protected by lawyers, religious radicals, and old money for some time now."

"Which is why we kill him now, set him ablaze like he almost did to this boy," Bain passionately suggested. Bain picked up the silver canister full of fuel, and dumped it in the grave. The liquid hit Lance in the face.

"Not yet," Kayden asked and gently pushed Bain away from the grave.

"What are you?" Bain asked.

Kayden looked into Bain's eyes intensely.

"I do not have an answer. All I can say is that, I know this is happening for a reason. And I know I can change things for the better."

"What are you going to do with him?" Cari asked.

Flashes of red and blue lights bounced off the trees and grass. Beams of hard white light cut through the woods, along voices by the dozens.

"The fucking cops!" Bain asked.

"I have a plan," Kayden said.

"The bastards will let him walk again, like you said. Right?"

"Not this time."

"What makes this any different?"

"Me," Kayden said.

"What?"

"This time, I make him the example."

The police responded to a loud crash. Twelve officers ran towards the sound with guns drawn. They passed through a heavily wooded area and into a clearing. The first thing they saw was the source of the commotion—an overturned Chevy Bronco. The vehicle was sitting wheels to the sky and missing the driver's side door. The truck rocked back and forth.

The next thing the police saw was a little boy wrapped up in a white cloth. They immediately tended to him.

"It's him. It's the Dansin kid!" and officer yelled to the troopers behind him.

They also found Lance Goodard, who was in serious pain. An emergency medical team fished him out of the grave and brought him into custody.

On the nearby highway, the black SUV filled with four armed vigilantes and one supernatural ex-physician was just another vehicle on the road.

COXIM VILLAGE, BRAZIL

Each face of the village shined in the moonlight. They all shared the same surrendering, folded expression while each one, even the toddlers, begged for freedom. Tied together in perfect rows by their hands or their necks, the villagers had been forced out of their homes and into the center of their own modest community. Two dozen gunmen, dressed to their eyes in black, held them all by gun point, speechlessly demanding that the detainees remain still. And there wasn't any authority within a hundred miles that could come to their rescue.

The fresh dead were gathered into two dark, military trucks. A man standing with the assistance of a rusted walking stick looked at each of the bodies from a safe distance. Pointing his cane fitted with a human foot bone for a handle, he directed the gunmen as to which truck the body would be thrown into. Underneath a straw farming hat, the director maintained elegant mannerisms as he sorted through the carcasses, regardless of his bloodstained T-shirt that hid under an oversized blazer.

But the man in charge of the bigger picture was Donar Gamule, a spiked, blonde-headed Hercules that chewed a cigar butt. Like a statue, he did not react when handed a polished silver briefcase.

"Donar, don't tell me you came all the way from Belarus without bringing me a bottle of Vodka," the Latin gentleman said, as he handed over the case. Donar scratched his scar that stretched from his right eye to his throat.

Donar was not concerned with the Latin man's tease, nor his casual, slime-ball dialect. Once the case was opened for him, the stacks of aged bills quickly swallowed Donar's attention.

"And you are certain I could not interest you in a few hard workers for the farms?" Donar asked.

"Они—рудники. Брат, они—рудники!" barked the man leaning on the cane, pointing his finger at Donar with authority.

The Latin negotiator laughed and wiped the sweat away. "What is the cripple bitching about?"

Donar answered the angry man in their mother tongue. Even after concluding their conversation, the man in the cane seemed just as outraged.

"So?" Donar asked.

"Slaves? I have too many. Get rid of them. Like the deal says. I want to get out of this clean, like my lady's ass."

"Likewise," Donar replied and nodded to one of his gunmen.

With an invisible quickness, the appointed gunmen forced a silenced handgun to the back of the Latin mobster's head and put a tiny hole completely through his brain. The detained onlookers could only pray for such a quick ending.

"Brother?" Donar yelled to the man with the cane.

Ignoring Donar, the crippled man continued to sift through the remains as they were shown to him.

"Ospi!" Donar tried again.

The cripple turned to look.

"Finish. We move!" Donar demanded.

Ospi Gamule, Donar's fraternal twin brother, sorted the last carcass and limped his way to a Jeep, cursing the ground before him.

A soldier, wearing a sword strapped to his back, swiftly approached Donar and stood, patient and soundless.

"Burn it. Let the suits have this trash," Donar gave his orders, which were immediatly executed.

The screams and cries reached a pinnacle level as a dozen two handfuls swordsmen displayed their long blades to the prisoners. With practiced precision, every last man, woman, and child was sent to their next life. What once was a home to a peaceful people would become their flaming graves, for no other reason than the land they picked to build their village upon. Land in that region had become ungoverned and could be bought and sold by a person of power.

There wasn't a better person to call upon to clean out the closet than Donar Gamule. Unfortunately for victims of mass genocide, Donar was having a busy year and the phone kept ringing. Whether it was businessmen in need of land or presidents and dictators trying to control the population, Donar didn't care. This was all a game to him. And he was only in it to tear off a piece for himself.

"My client deserves his freedom until proven guilty."

"Your client is being charged with over two dozen counts of murder!"

"Falsely. And not the first time either. We've been here before. It's the same false story over and over again."

The courtroom was on fire. Members of the press, families of lost victims, men and women of the law all barked, chanted, threatened at the top of their lungs. The armed officers moved closer to the judge, wondering if the honorable judge would make it out alive.

It only took two days of confinement for Lance Goodard to get an arraignment in hopes of convincing a judge to allow him to leave his cell on bond. Half the world wanted him dead. And not just any death. A slow and painful death. The other half found it to be some kind of conspiracy. They knew Lance Goodard as a man of great faith. Extreme at times, of course, but simply not capable of the charges against him. Twenty-nine counts of kidnapping, all of child victims under the age of twelve.

Lance sat in a dark blue jump suit, hands cuffed to a chain around his feet; unshaven, exhausted, but allowing the courtroom to see his perky demeanor. He even had a slight grin, before his attorney told him to get rid of it. His attorney dressed in a pinstriped three piece suit, as if he wouldn't dare step out into the ring without a little style. His shoes shined like glass as he galloped around the stage, aiming to convince the judge, like he had done several times before.

The prosecution lashed out with violent tones. They were out for blood.

The judge appeared overworked and uninspired. He wanted it over, quickly.

"That is correct. This is not the first time. This is the third time Mr. Goodard has been accused of a capital offense," the prosecutor continued.

"Accused, but later disproven. Released by the hands of justice, twice," Lance's attorney struck back.

"Those cases are still under review."

As they argued back and forth, the guard outside of the courthouse was somehow relieved of his weapons and knocked unconscious, allowing for five people to pass by without quarrel.

"Your honor. My client deserves his rights. He deserves to be set free until the day of this trial, just like anyone else. Lance Goodard is not a threat to society. He is a public servant, preaching the Bible, offering the people an alternative to crime. The defense will prove that this is clearly a liberal conspiracy to taint my client's reputation and send an innocent man to the chair. Now, are we going to undermine true American legislation? The Constitution? Only to inhibit my client of his God given rights?"

"The man was found with a kidnapped victim."

"Correct. But the prosecution is not being descriptive enough. My client was found with a kidnapped victim, severely injured and inside a six-foot hole in the ground. Does this sound like you found a murderer?"

"Why doesn't your client make a statement? Why is he so quiet? What really happened, Mr. Goodard?" the prosecutor spoke directly towards Lance at the other table.

"The devil showed his face—" Lance began to shout at the members of the courtroom before his attorney shut him up.

"My client is practicing his fifth amendment rights today," the attorney shook his head at Lance, ordering him not to speak.

Just outside of the courtroom, the two guards at the door reached for their pistols, but did not get the opportunity to use them. Instead their guns were somehow dismantled into several pieces of useless steel and discarded. The officers retreated.

"Your honor. We cannot afford to let Lance Goodard walk. For any bail. There is enough evidence gathered on this charge alone to consider Lance Goodard a danger to society, without even looking at his history," the prosecutor stated.

"That's enough!" the judge slammed down his gavel, ending the discussion and silencing the crowd. "The fact of the matter is the child has been found unharmed. Mr. Lance Goodard was found in a ditch, injured. He was found by an anonymous phone call. Those are the facts so far. There is nothing that leads me to believe that he will be putting any lives in danger by leaving this courtroom until his trial. His past is inadmissible."

The judge rubbed his head and scribbled on a document before him. "Bail is set at $20,000," he declared, and began to rise.

The double doors of the courtroom blew open as if by an invisible monsoon. Kayden Archer and his four followers appeared. At once, all of the seating benches broke free from the courtroom floor and levitated straight up into the air, sending the audience members to their feet and knees. The double doors slammed shut. The two tables occupied by Lance's representation and the prosecutors rose up into the air. Papers floated to the ground. With unearthly speed, the tables flew past Kayden and pressed firmly against the double doors to provide a blockade. The benches flew against the windows, blocking out the sun.

Not one member of the courtroom remained calm. Each of them either screamed or cursed. They forced themselves against the walls cursing all in sight. Bain and the others kept their positions near the double doors, armed heavily. The only person that kept his seat was Lance Goodard, who nearly fell into shock as he watched the laws of nature deteriorate around him.

Kayden calmly marched forward. The room had fallen silent enough to hear Kayden's boot heels beat against the floor. His facial expression let the crowd know of his irritation, and his tall, confident stride made them all aware of the grasp he had on the entire courtroom.

"What good is a road that has no lines, nor indication of where it will lead? One that is full of holes and cracks? What good is a road that has no law? What good is fruit that grows from dead soil? That has no sun. That drinks from poisoned water?" Kayden strolled around the courtroom, eyeing every fearful attendee, every cop, the judge, the attorneys. "What good is a law, if it has no backbone? What good is a law if wealth can persuade it? What good is a law if one can dodge it using a loophole fabricated from thin air? What good is YOUR law?"

Photographers took advantage of the opportunity to snap several shots of Kayden. Reporters kept their recorders on.

"Your system is flawed...corrupt...and no longer reliable!"

Kayden roared. The wood in the room seemed to shake from his voice alone. The two flags posted on either side of the judge's stand— a United States flag and a Pennsylvania State flag—left their bases and stabbed into the floor like spears nearly three feet part from one another, directly in front of Lance Goodard

"There was a time when the punishment fit the crime, when regular people took on the responsibility of rectifying the situation. There was a time when criminals would actually consider the consequences of their actions. Now look at the world. Look at him."

Kayden pointed at Lance Goodard, who wasn't even willing to look Kayden in the eyes. Without warning, his restraints broke away from Lance. Even with his hands and legs free, Lance couldn't find the courage to stand.

"A man that has taken child after child, for no other reason than to fulfill a sick crusade. A demented serial killer with all the support he needed. The church, an institution we as people put at the highest moral plateau, has provided Mr. Goodard with shelter, money, a stage, and when he is caught red-handed, they throw him a gold-studded lawyer to whittle the chains loose."

"What is happening here?" the judge, standing motionless, growled at Kayden. Kayden turned and smiled at the judge.

"Right. More action, less chat. Your honor, I apologize for the digression," Kayden returned.

Kayden reached out with one hand towards the prosecutor

and the other hand towards Lance's attorney. Their belts unbuckled and left their pants. Kayden caught both belts with each hand. Lance awkwardly rose to his feet, as if he had no control over his actions. Tossing about unwillingly, Lance ended up with each hand holding the two flag poles protruding from the floor. Kayden walked to Lance and tied each hand firmly to each pole. Lance let his fear ring out with screams.

"I would like to reintroduce a form of punishment that perhaps will make those who seek a life of crime to question their actions, *before* the innocent become victims."

The whole room watched as Kayden retrieved a six-ounce canister full of a yellowish liquid from the pocket of his trench coat. With an eye dropper, Kayden laid a drop of the liquid on each inner forearm of Lance Goodard.

"For now on, the world shall fear the consequences." (The whole room watched as Kayden retrieved a six-ounce canister full of a yellowish liquid from the pocket of his trench coat.) Until the early hours of the morning, Kayden worked to concoct a unique formula using the diseased blood of his pervious adversary -Armand.

Kayden shoved the canister inside Lance's mouth and poured the liquid down his throat.

"See with your own eyes what happens to those who lead an immoral life."

Lance looked to his right arm. His skin began to turn yellow, then red, then dark red. An open sore formed within seconds. The skin on his arm began to deteriorate.

Women screamed.

"This is the new era of justice!" Kayden concluded.

Lance's other arm had the same reaction. A fast, flesh eating infection seemed to eat him alive. Shortly after the infection exposed the muscle tissue and bone of both his arms, his screams turned into gargling sounds. In seconds, his throat and chest tissue became exposed.

Kayden watched his work progress with the same infuriated expression on his face. Before Lance's skin completely disappeared, Kayden walked towards the door. The pews fell from the windows and tables fell from the doors. The crowd maneuvered away from Kayden. With a strong boot, Kayden kicked the double doors open. Bain, satisfied and committed, followed Kayden proudly. Gar, Cari, and Alton joined them. The doors slammed shut behind them.

When Lance Goodard took his last breath, Kayden took his tenth step down a wide hallway toward the city streets. The instant Lance died, Kayden's vision left him. He stopped his pace and went to his knees, rubbing his eyes.

"Archer? What's happening? Archer?" Bain asked, looking around the hallway for cops to show up with guns blazing. He knew damn well Kayden was their only real line of defense.

Kayden's vision came back to him. He looked around the hallway, confused. One of the doors further down the hallway opened. Lance Goodard, half eaten, insides exposed, appeared in the doorway yelling. Lance ran towards the five of them as if to attack. Gar and Bain opened fire on Lance. The bullets went right through him, putting half a dozen bullet holes and shotgun blasts into the walls behind Lance. Before Lance was close enough to attack, he vanished right before their eyes.

"What in the hell was that?" Gar hollered. Gar looked back into the courtroom to see the crowd escaping through the exits. The rest of Lance Goodard's body hung from the two flag poles. "You saw that right?" Gar asked Bain.

"We all did." Cari stated, trying to get Kayden back on his feet.

Down the hallway, another door opened to reveal an old acquaintance. It was a man, soaking wet, covered in chains. His skin was pale white and his eyeballs had been plucked out. Kayden nearly fainted when he saw his face. It was Jack Kootz, aka Budge. He dragged a chain with a weight attached across the floor toward Kayden.

"I am of God. Not you," Budge spoke.

Again, the swarm of bullets did nothing to Budge. He disappeared just as he came close enough to touch Kayden.

JUSTIN TREECE

From the other end of the hallway, another old friend appeared. His body was badly burned. Only half of his face was visible. But it was enough for Kayden to recognize him. It was his second victim, the murderer of his wife, only known by his alias—Armand.

Armand marched toward Kayden. His charred skin flaked away as he walked. When he neared Kayden, he spoke.

"I am his servant. Not you."

Another skeletal version of Lance appeared standing right next to Alton. Alton freaked and backed into Kayden.

"God has given me power. Not you."

Lance took a swing at Alton. The skeleton hand went straight through Alton, leaving him unharmed.

"Someone want to tell me what the fuck is going on?" Bain hollered.

"It's him." Alton pointed to Kayden. "He's making this shit happen."

Immediately, Kayden was convinced that Alton was correct.

"You are making us hallucinate. You have to be," said Alton.

Kayden nodded. He knew it. Alton was absolutely correct. His thoughts were projecting themselves before his very own eyes, as well as those around him. Every mental image that went through Kayden's mind was projected to all those within close proximity. After the execution, he had subconsciously cycled through his killings from Budge, to Armand, to Lance Goodard. His free subconscious had fabricated the rest. Unfortunately for those that shared the same area, they too were forced to experience the fabrications of Kayden's mind.

"Get a grip on yourself man. There is going to be an army outside waiting to take us all down," Bain demanded.

He was right.

The five of them stepped out from the courthouse entrance, down a flight of marble stairs and into the street. Market Street had already been blocked off by a swarm of city cop cars. At least a dozen officers pointed their rifles and handguns at the five targets. Behind the cop cars, three S.W.A.T. team vans pulled up and unloaded twenty-four heavily armed agents. The gunmen took positions behind the cop cars. Down the opposite side of the street was a three way intersection. If they could make a run for it, and dodge the onslaught of bullets, they might have had a chance.

"Put your weapons down. Get on your knees with your hands behind your head," a voice behind a megaphone ordered.

The five of them stood frozen, unsure of their next move. Surrounding them was nothing but skyscrapers and concrete. Their one and only vehicle was a block behind an army of the Philadelphia Police. They were trapped.

Kayden heard an officer yell, "Take 'em down!"

When he heard this, the three black S.W.A.T. team vans left the ground and climbed thirty feet in the air. The vans twirled in midair, landing on their sides just feet in front of Kayden, just in time to catch a swarm of bullets intended for Kayden and his group. With a temporary shield, they had a few seconds to think of a way out.

"Thanks and all that, but these assholes are gonna be on top of us any minute. You have a plan for that?" Alton asked Kayden.

Kayden avoided the question. It was obvious that he had no clue.

"Whatever it is, you better do it now," Gar suggested.

Kayden, out of options and partially expecting another Lance Goodard to appear, looked to the sky for answers. Strangely enough, by looking at the skyscrapers that blocked out the sun, a solution came to him.

The leading officer of the S.W.A.T., slightly stunned by the unnatural events unfolding before his eyes, as well as the intelligence he had received only minutes prior, signaled his troops to move forward and advance on the fortress of overturned vans. Their formation proceeded without opposition.

Light footed, six of the two dozen law enforcers came within inches of the vehicles.

"Heads!"

One of the officers shouted, allowing each of the advancing gunmen to halt and look to the sky, only to become bewildered by yet another freak occurrence.

One Liberty Place was a sixty-one story skyscraper shaped like a mountain, with layers on top of layers of steel and glass and at the highest point of the structure was a sharp antenna tower. As the officers looked up, the tip of the skyscraper began to lean towards the city street and over the heads of the S.W.A.T. team.

Eyes opened wide as windows of the base levels of One Liberty Place began to explode, sending glass onto the street and on top of the frozen officers. The sounds emitted were, perhaps, comparable to an ocean liner bending in half.

Inevitably, the structure of the building failed. The top third of the building broke apart and came crashing toward the ground, right on top of the law enforcers.

The sounds of horrified, retreating lawmen filled Market Street as the towers crashed down on them. Some of them hit the ground, covering their heads. Some just lifted an arm to shield their faces. All of them understood there was no escape. This was the end for them.

Dust and debris rushed through the city streets. Those that were not in the direct path of the fallen skyscraper ran from the wreckage. In seconds, the entire street was suffocated by clouds of thick dust and ash. With no clear line of sight, people collided with one another as they tried to find an escape. Injured cops crawled along the ground, screaming for help or an end. Police sirens and megaphones sounded off as the survivor rescue effort went into effect immediately.

Gar held Cari tightly. They were both on their knees embracing. They hid their faces from the clouds of dust. Both Alton and Bain had mashed themselves inside the overturned vehicles the very second the tower collapsed. Kayden was nowhere in sight.

"Where is he?" Bain cried out.

"No idea," Alton.

Something beat on the roof of the truck Alton and Bain took cover in. The sound was like the heel of a boot.

Inside the truck, a wind channeled through and sent all of the dust and ash out of the truck. Bain looked out the windshield to see all of the dust clouds disappear around the overturned trucks. Gar and Cari became visible. They opened their eyes to see the sky, the buildings, and Kayden standing tall atop one of the trucks.

The four vigilantes climbed up to join Kayden. They all were daunted by what they witnessed on top of that car. Before them were grown men and women crawling around in agony, searching for safety. No fire. No dust. No ash. No debris. Just men and women suffering for no reason whatsoever.

"What happened to the wreckage?" Bain asked.

Kayden pointed to the sky. One Liberty Place was standing tall and intact.

"I don't understand," Cari said.

"They see...what I want them to see," Kayden proudly announced.

Not in any harm's way. Not in any real pain at all, the city street was filled with people fighting for their lives from a shared hallucination. Kayden had created a new world for them to experience, one in which an enormous skyscraper had just fallen on their heads. None of it was fact. They all were racing away from a fictitious catastrophe.

A second squad of S.W.A.T. team arrived from the other end of the street. Seven vans full of gunmen came to a screeching halt fifty yards from Kayden. The lawmen immediately jumped out and assumed a defensive position.

Kayden took one look in their direction.

Fire, like a tidal wave of ignited fuel, poured into the city street from all cracks, alleyways, and side streets. The fire moved faster than lava would from a volcanic eruption, but with the same temperature and destructive force. The side street vendors melted. Smaller buildings were drowned in fire. All that was in the path of the flames incinerated instantly.

The S.W.A.T. team surrendered their positions and took cover as the flames closed in on them. Just like their hallucinating co-workers on the other end of the street, they had given up all hope on survival.

Seconds before all the suited lawmen were smothered in flames, the fire disappeared. The gunmen looked up to see clear skies and One Liberty Place still standing. Every cop, firefighter, press agent, and pedestrian opened their eyes to see that their worries were over. Some questioned if they were still alive. Some thought they had entered the afterlife. Yet, they all rose to their feet unharmed. No one spoke. They let their eyes float around the city street, waiting for hell to return and the struggle to continue.

After a few minutes of complete disorientation, the city rejoiced once they knew they were safe. This catastrophic event they had endured had been a hoax of some unbelievable entity, capable of fooling an entire packed city street. Cops hugged one another and wiped their tears away, thankful that they still had their lives.

Kayden and his followers did not stick around to join the festivities. The wanted, supernatural fugitives simply drove out of the city as free men and women. The first conversation between them, one that would begin heated debate, started with Alton asking the simple question,

"So what do we do now?"

By his smirk above his squared chin, Kayden had seemed to have a plan already in mind.

"There is the one...now this is two."

Deacon James rambled to himself as he put one foot in front of the other. He had never walked so fast in his life.

"Three, three must be bigger. Someone bigger."

The students walking to and from class watched the Deacon as he breezed by. Mostly because of his clerical attire, but also because of how he conversed with himself all the way to the doorway of the Liberal Arts building. Inside he focused on the numbers assigned to each classroom, repeating each number as he marched by.

When he found his destination, he did not hesitate to open the door and let himself inside. The class was full of alert college students and a teacher that was in middle of lecture.

"May I help you?" the offended teacher blurted at the priest.

"Grace Archer. Grace Archer. The sister. The sister," the Deacon vaguely explained and peered around the room, looking at each young face.

"Grace? Do you know what this about?" the teacher asked, looking toward the back of the classroom.

Grace pulled her head from her notepad and stood up straight.

"Miss Archer. Miss Archer," Deacon James said, seeming relieved to see her, "Can... I speak to you? Speak for a while. Please? Please?"

Deacon James tried to calm himself and breathe, but it was no use. He was frantic.

Grace left her things and slowly made her way to the front of the class. The teacher approached her and whispered, kindly asking her if everything was alright. Grace nodded and left the classroom with Deacon James.

Outside of the classroom, he took three, loud, deep breaths. Once he caught his breath, he spoke to Grace.

"When we spoke the other day, you asked me if I would turn in someone I loved for doing something criminal," the Deacon's words were rushed, but nonetheless made sense.

Grace nodded and looked away, nervously. It was obvious that she did not want to continue the conversation.

"I believe it is you who must right your brother's wrong. No handcuffs, nor jail, nor law can help him now. It is you and I that must help him."

"Deacon, I know you are trying to help, but you sound crazy right now," Grace touched his arm, offering her sympathy.

"No. No. No. Grace. Please. You have to understand. This is much bigger than you think. The news, they have it all wrong. They are masking the truth because it seems unbelievable. But you must see past it. You must find the truth."

"News? What news?" Grace asked.

"Evil has found a way through. A prophecy has been reborn. You must listen to me," Deacon James leaned down to look her dead in the face.

"Deacon James, stop this! Stop it. I can't deal with this right now. I just can't. Please leave me," Grace tossed her hands up in frustration. But before she could finish her reply and get back to her studies, she was interrupted by two fellow students in the hallway.

"Grace. We just saw the news. Nuts. Your brother just kicked some ass. You haven't talked to him, have you?" one of the kids asked.

Grace looked back at the Deacon.

"Did you hear how everyone downtown says there was some kind of terrorist attack, but nobody knows what is going on? It's absolutely insane," said the other student.

Without offering a reply, Grace walked swiftly towards the media lab around the corner. Inside, a small cluster of students were staring upwards at a screen mounted on the wall. A reporter blasted the facts of what appeared to be a serious national concern.

Grace's jaw dropped and her eyes began to water when her family photo, taken only months ago, appeared on the screen. The image was zoomed in on her brother, Kayden. The details of the report brought the sweat from Grace's brow. Her brother was a fugitive for a crime that he most certainly did commit. Numerous eyes, cameras, and other forms of evidence clearly pointed the finger at Kayden Archer. Grace was not overly concerned about the unexplained, unearthly events took place during the downtown episode. She was mainly bothered by the fact that the next time she would see her brother would most likely be behind bars or in a casket. The rest just sounded like rubbish.

She turned and squeezed Deacon James, holding on while she let the tears fall on his clerical garb.

"We haven't the time to fret. There is much I have to tell you. You are not ready. The world is not ready. But we have no time. No time at all."

But Grace let go of him and ran. She stopped for nothing, not even the screams from Deacon James, or her friends and classmates who tried to stop her. She needed to be with the ones she loved and trusted. She needed to be home.

The traffic lights did not matter. The stop signs did not matter. The rules. The laws. The traditions. Nothing mattered to her, except for her vehicle to get her to her home. To her family. To her mother.

But a woman whose heart had been ripped out and stepped on by the same news channel coverage would hardly be any help to the situation. Alice Archer was a mother of two, faithful to the Lord, loving wife, and a servant of those in need. She spent years of her life traveling to different parts of the world to feed the starving and cure the sick. She assumed that the Lord would be merciful to her and her loved ones.

She was wrong. The television showed her son on camera murdering a prisoner of the law in a courtroom. The footage showed her a very different man than the one she had raised. A man with phenomenal power. A man with hate. A man above the laws of man or God.

"Your system is flawed…corrupt…and no longer reliable!"

The footage shown across the world allowed viewers to hear the voice of the fugitive. Alice Archer listened carefully, yet she did not recognize the voice. This was a different boy from the one she had loved and nurtured.

Richard Archer leaned against the wall, speechless. There

was no hope in conjuring an explanation for the images on the screen. Richard was thrown apart after watching squads of cops and pedestrians crawl in the street and beg for their lives from an invisible enemy. He tried to convince himself that it this was a well done, fallacious attempt at trickery. Had it been anyone else than the son of his wife, he would have turned his attention immediately. But that was his boy, in front of the world, taking on the law. There wasn't a reasonable reaction to what Alice and Richard Archer watched unfold on their screen. So they didn't react.

When Grace burst through the front door, both her mom and dad jumped. They embraced in the doorway, like parents protecting the last remaining young. The women cried while Richard swallowed his tears. He wouldn't dare unglue himself from the television screen.

Grace told her parents how Deacon Gregory James had pulled her out of class to tell her the news. Richard explained how the Deacon had stopped by the Archer's home to look for Grace. He described his behavior as delirious and terrified.

"He went on about prophecy. And how it must be stopped," Richard explained.

Grace shouted through her tears," Turn it off. Please turn it off!"

Richard went to the television and mashed the off button, but the screen would not click off. Richard cursed the television and mashed the rest of the buttons. The screen passed through several channels, all of which were covering the downtown Philly incident. He let the television sit on a British station that was not covering the story.

To their surprise, Deacon James approached the Archer's family doorway. He didn't even bother to knock before twisting the doorknob. Grace detached herself from her mother and fled to the other side of the living room when she saw the Deacon's trembling eyes.

Richard stopped the clergyman before he fully entered the

home. "Greg, I'm sorry, but this just isn't the time. I'm gonna have to ask you to come by another day."

"No. Please. There isn't any time. We have to stop it. Please listen to me," the Deacon begged.

"Now Deacon, I am not going to tell you again. Please leave. We, as a family, must deal with this ourselves."

"I agree! Let me help you do so."

Richard gently moved the Deacon's fifty-something-year-old body off of his porch. The Deacon offered no challenge, physically. Richard walked him all the way to the fence and onto the sidewalk.

"Richard. You have to listen to me. I can explain all of this." Deacon James pleaded.

Richard moved to close the gate in front of him. As he did, the Deacon noticed a silhouette of a person falling from inside the house.

He yelled, pointing "Richard!"

Alice Archer's mind had completely left her. She hit the ground unconscious. Richard ran towards his wife. The Deacon followed.

Grace screamed and went to her knees by her mother's frozen body. Richard pulled Alice into his lap and immediately attempted to awaken her.

The Deacon did not assist or witness the aid given to Mrs. Archer. His attention was focused on the screen the moment he entered the room and heard the news report being given.

"...although no remains have been found... South American billionaire CEO Marquez Domini turned over information regarding the series of disappearances of almost a quarter of a million people in the Southern Brazilian region...upset by his missing son who co-operated CoNam...the two brothers are wanted for questioning...Domini has publicly stated his intent to seek out the brothers and turn them over to the authorities."

On the screen were photographs of two men: a large, blonde man with a militant glare and a pale-skinned cripple hiding under a straw hat.

"I told him." Alice Archer snapped to life, yelling to her husband's face.

Richard, thankful to see her alive, rocked her to back and forth to try and calm her.

"I told him who is father was. I'm sorry. He had to know," Alice cried.

She pointed at the screen. Once she did, she dropped her pointed finger and reached for her arm. Pain struck her hard. Her face poured anguish. Richard responded by setting her down. He ordered Grace to call for help.

GLASYA-LABOLAS

RUSSO AIRSTRIP
EASTERN PENNSYLVANIA

Why are we hiding? Do we really need to hide?" Gar gave up whispering and spoke at a casual volume.

"It's better to stay under the radar," Alton kept his whisper, trying to encourage Gar to do the same.

The two were crouched in shrubbery along the outer perimeters of a busy airstrip. Dark camouflaged military planes occupied the runway along with the occasional Learjet.

Ten yards away from the two bickering men, Kayden stood tall as he watched the airstrip closely. Cari and Bain, leaning against a couple trees, held their weapons at their chest.

"What's the plan for getting us inside, Archer? They will spot us the second we approach that fence. The military doesn't sleep. You hear me, mate?" Bain asked.

Ignoring Bain's concern, Kayden concentrated on nothing but the next step. There was no turning back; no time for proper planning. This was it. This was his fate.

A monster of an aircraft with four massive engines arrived at the airstrip and shut down in the middle of the runway.

"It's a C-130. I've fallen out of a few of those before," Gar explained to Alton.

Gar had a fairly extensive knowledge on military craft, especially the C-130 that just landed. Its purpose was to transport large supplies and entire armies. Everyone watched as a camouflaged Hummer drove into the cargo exit of the aircraft.

"I have a mate that might give us a lift. Lets sleep this off and—" Bain began his plea, but was cut off by Kayden.

"You will want to find some other place to stand."

The ground shook like a bomb had landed only feet away. Cari looked around to find the source. A hundred yards away and closing fast was a massive boulder that looked to have been dislodged from the side of a mountain. It crushed the ground and the trees that stood, leaving an indention as it bounced directly towards them.

Bain and Cari took off in separate directions. The bolder cleared Kayden's head by mere inches. The rock collided with the Earth two more times before smashing into the security fence, creating a considerable gap in the line. The boulder stopped only a few feet after crushing the fence, although the momentum it carried would suggest it should have continued its destructive path all the way to the airstrip.

Calmly, Kayden walked toward the parked C-130.

Richard Archer allowed Deacon James to drive the family vehicle to the emergency room after Alice's chest pains progressed. The Deacon continued to force his voice, even while Richard tried to comfort his ill wife. Grace, in the front seat, actually took an ear to half of what the clergyman was trying to explain as he sped through the neighborhood roads.

At the hospital, Alice was immediately diagnosed with respiratory failure, which had led to the heart attack. The staff performed the required tests and medicated her. Eventually she was sedated and laid down in a hospital bed, where her husband and daughter sat at her side.

Deacon James stood in the doorway of Alice's room for what seemed like hours before giving up his attempt at trying to have a conversation with the Archer's. His words blew by them like dust. But within a few minutes after he left, Grace began to think on him. The Deacon ranted until his voice went horse, speaking of a prophecy that involved Kayden. Grace, a fairly researched follower of Christ, had never heard such a story at mass or when listening to her mother's interpretations. To hear this entangled, haunting tale uttered by a man of the cloth, and with such conviction, was hard to completely ignore.

Grace left her mother's side to search for the Deacon. She found him kneeling in the hospital chapel. In the dark, ten-seat room of worship, Gregory's head hung low on his folded hands.

Grace picked up a Bible that sat on one of the white painted wooden pews. She brought it with her as she approached the Deacon.

"I've read this thing since I was a little girl. There is nothing in it that describes whatever it is you are talking about," Grace startled him with her entrance.

Gregory James looked at her with borderline sinister eyes, saturated with frustration. Her condescending tone boiled him to the point that he ripped the Bible from her grasp and slung it into the corner, bouncing it off the wall hard enough to leave a mark.

"Those pages are hardly a fraction of the story. In that book are the parts the feeble-minded can handle. Exposing the rest would only fuel the fire with the remains of the dead. Which is exactly what...it wants."

Grace's turned her offense into defense. The Deacon's sinister demeanor poured fresh fear into her heart. And she needed to know why.

"Show me," she requested.

He did just that.

What separated Deacon James from the rest of his peers, and the majority of the Roman Catholic Church, was his devotion to history. With any topic—rather it was politics, war, health, or religion—the Deacon needed to see the roots of the issue before any assumptions or queries were made. Not only did he need to clearly see how events developed, he needed to dissect each ingredient from start to finish. Most men of the cloth spent their time with the community, offering guidance to their followers. Deacon James spent his time in books, historical archives, discussion forums, and even conspiracy theories that attacked Christianity and other faiths. Sadly, his research had taken him away from all the fruits of life, excluding him from any enjoyment for much of the fifty-four years he had spent on the Earth. He alienated himself from a family that did not share his dedication. Instead, his breaths were for God, and nothing else.

Quite the contrast from a twenty-two year old college girl, who patiently accepted the world around her and rarely hesitated to take advantage of what pleasures were offered. Grace Archer considered herself a Christian, but, unlike most who celebrated her religion, she stoutly admitted to not being Christ-like. She believed the stories in the Bible to be true, although she had never read the book in its entirety. She was independent enough to question all the she had been taught, but had enough love in her heart and a strong acknowledgement of the creativity in nature to truly believe in God. To have a faith that allowed for a reasonable explanation for her life, gave her a reason to pursue enjoyment and progress simultaneously.

Having the curtain drawn on a matter that affected not only the fundamentals of her existence but her family as well, was difficult to swallow.

As a man in his early twenties, Deacon James's studies dove deeply into the documentation excluded from the published Bible and written during the same period as the New Testament Scripture. Of the several staggering, unheard stories he uncovered, one in particular stayed in a dark closet of his memory banks for decades.

At some unknown date during the first few centuries, a document predicting a dark prophecy had been recorded and signed by a man named Shudagon. From what little information the Deacon could gather on the creation of the document, the found that the text was handwritten with blood on animal skin, known by many enthusiasts to be secured by The Vatican. Rumors were spread that the document was the one and only writing Shudagon had ever made, which led his peers to believe that his body had been used by dark forces to establish the prophecy upon the Earth. Numerous copies had circulated in the underground, which fell into the hands of the Deacon during his much younger years, which sparked an invested interest.

The prophecy outlined a strategic plot for the allegiance of all evil to win the war against God. Very much mimicking the role of Jesus Christ, the prophecy would bring forth a son of Hell. The son would be forced on a quest that would ultimately transform him into a minion of the purest, most ancient form of evil. With unstoppable powers, Minion—a name used in the prophecy—would be able to recreate the world as Hell sought fit.

To bring forth the prophecy, a human son would be born from an act of violence. He would live the life of a common man until the time came for evil to impose its guidance. At that time, the son would unknowingly be sent on a hellish crusade to track down and kill four demonically processed humans. As each damned soul is killed by the hands of the prophesized son, the son will inherit a supernatural power. These powers will be unstoppable by any mortal and will ultimately aid in the transformation of the prophesized son into Minion.

Those that have been fortunate enough to study the prophecy understand that if the son of hell tracks down and kills the four damned souls, his powers will complete his transformation and bring forth hell on Earth.

"A son born from an act of violence?" Grace asked the Deacon as he explained.

"Yes."

"What does that mean?"

"Rape. The son will conceived by rape."

Grace shivered at the thought."And this son of hell, Minion, wouldn't know he was a part of this prophecy?"

"Of course not. This theory is buried so deeply that I, myself, could be the only one alive that is aware of its existence. If it were me, and I developed these powers, I would assume I was being gifted by God."

Grace shook her head. In her eyes, the Deacon was narrating some horrified, magical, biblical tale. Yet he told it with so much conviction that she became completely fascinated. Her perception wrestled back and forth between being completely focused on the Deacons story, and hysterical for paying any attention to what could be a silly fable, made up by bored biblical scholars.

"What is so special about these four people and why would they need to be killed? Wouldn't Hell want as many evil people spread out in the world?"

"First off, when you think of God, or the Devil, do you see them as human?"

"I put a face on them. I seem them as having a human form."

"As many do, but I do not. I know God as a source of energy present in the world, influencing the path, feeding off of love, kindness, and generosity. God has neither hands nor feet. He is everywhere."

"Well, sure. That's kind of the idea."

"This concept is very important if we are to understand the conflict between good and evil. Hell surrounds us in the same way. Influencing us all, feeding on hate, destruction, pain, and fear. The war against heaven and hell is actually a fight over the energy that exists in the world. Both sides are smart, unrelenting, and immortal. Each trying to win our souls to become stronger."

"So this prophecy is sort of like Hell's revenge for the prophecy of Christ?"

"Exactly."

"That still doesn't answer my question. Why have this son kill evil people? Wouldn't they want to have them around?"

"Grace, I don't have all the answers. In the end, I'm just a student. If I was to guess, I would say that evil is putting their son to the test, so they have set up obstacles for their son to endure. If he passes the test, he will truly be their chosen son. Or, maybe they have set up human canisters of evil energy that their son must open and absorb. Maybe it's both. I really don't know. It boggles me as well. The Lord works in mysterious ways, and so does his foe."

Grace knew the Deacon was suggesting that this son of Hell was, in fact, her very brother, Kayden. He had been hinting to the idea all day. But Grace was not convinced.

"So who are these four people this Minion will go after?"

The Deacon retrieved a folded, white sheet of paper from his pocket and opened it for Grace. The page was a copy of the original recorded document of the prophecy, known by those aware of its existence as the Shudagon Prophecy. The text was written in some ancient, Hebraic language she was completely unfamiliar with, but somehow seeing the text anchored the Deacon's story. The Deacon translated the document for her.

As the prophecy stated, the four targets the son would pursue were men possessed by four specific demons. In Hell, these demons acted as the facilitators of the damned.

The first of the four will be possessed by the demon Zepar. In Hell, Zepar's kingdom of sexual slavery serves as the brothel for all the lords and ranked guardians. Zepar will exhibit himself as an admirer of the human female form, yet his true intentions are to drain from her all the life and wealth available. He will take advantage of his seductive characteristics in the most malevolent ways. Ultimately, he will live to destroy women.

"At our first meeting, you mentioned your brother had taken a life out of revenge for his wife's death. When I asked you if the life he had taken belonged to his wife's lover, you nodded—yes," the Deacon said.

Again, Grace nodded.

The Deacon waited for a response, but Grace kept quiet.

"I shall continue," he said.

The Deacon described the second demon—The Demon Moloch. Moloch was an outcast tyrant of Hell. Never committed to his chosen role, Moloch expressed his eternal yearning to be next to God as His son. More so than any of the damned, Moloch resented Christ for being the son of the Almighty. He declared Christ as his enemy and unworthy to behold the word of God. On Earth, Moloch will spread the word of God throughout the lands in his own unique interpretation. He will have no hesitation to commit any sin that he understands to be of assistance to God, regardless of the consequences. Moloch turns the word of God against itself to develop his own kingdom of Anti-Christ.

"You are aware of the man your brother killed inside the courtroom? Lance Goodard?"

"Very little. Only what was on the news. He was some kind of priest? That kidnapped children? The cops caught him in a field with the Paul Dansin kid. Thank God he is back home safe."

"Yes. Thank God, or thank your brother. Lance Goodard was not much of priest, more like a lunatic. I have listened to him speak. His ideas were that of a misguided soul, begging to ignite a new theology. He was obsessed with the innocence of children and how their lack of sin would somehow aid in our struggle against evil. If these rumors are true, he has single handedly sacrificed numerous children for this misguided idea. As a man that has served God for all my years, I can gladly say his damned soul is where it belongs."

"So sad," Grace gasped.

"I suppose your brother found out what this monster had done and decided to make him into an example."

"It doesn't make any sense. My brother would never—"

"Let us not forget the influence evil has on the world. It can pull even the most righteous soul into darkness without the soul even being aware of what is happening. That is evil's most effective strategy—to become invisible. If we do not believe in its power, evil is free to act as it may without obstacle."

"Even if evil really exists, good will always have the upper hand," she said.

"And why do you think that?"

"Because we have survived for a long time. If evil was so dangerous, we would have been long gone years ago, right?"

"This is a much different era we live in. It is much easier to mistake comfort with sin. It is much easier to confuse progress with sin. We falsely claim our judgments on others as God's word. Our successes are often at the expense of the poor or weak. We've taken his way and turned it upside down, and somehow called it Christianity. And whose plan do you think that was?"

Grace bowed her head.

"Do you think capitalism and Christianity come together in harmony?"

Grace did not answer.

"Of course not. Do you think we should go into battle with other parts of the world to defend something like capitalism? Do you think we should kill in the name of God?"

Grace's expression showed a slight hint of trust in Gregory's words.

"Absolutely not. This is Hell's plan. All of it. Disguised to look as if it is God's work. And, if I do say so, an ingenious plan. This prophecy couldn't have come at a better time. For Minion can think he is on a crusade in God's name, when really is bringing forth our extinction."

Grace had a moment of clarity. She was starting to peel back her foundations and really take a deep look inside herself, as well as the rest of mankind.

"And the last two?" she asked.

"The last two of the possessed are spawned from the same seed. Glasya-Labolas is the name of the damned. When the demon crossed into hell, he was split in half for his soul was too hateful to be contained as one. Glasya's passion is for war. Constant battles are fought for no other reason than for Glasya's entertainment. The more blood is shed, the more powerful his kingdom becomes."

"Labolas is the master of all the dark arts such as masochism, mesmerism, ritual, and even biological art. He breathes for nothing but creative expression in its most sinister, contemptible form. His inspiration is pain and the oats of free will. His canvas aligns his path. His tools become anything he acquires."

"Glasya-Labolas represents the most ungraceful form of existence. Life means nothing, death is captivating. All compassion is lost."

"Horrible," Grace said.

"It truly is."

"Does this prophecy talk about these powers that the Minion will get as he kills these guys?"

"It does not. Not in the slightest. The prophecy merely states that he will obtain powers. It does not describe his abilities. What it does detail are some ground rules that actually work in our favor, and give us a chance to stop this before it's too late."

"For instance, if any of the four possessed souls were to ask God for forgiveness, the prophecy is voided, for Christ has allowed us eternal forgiveness of any sin *if* forgiveness is asked for. If either of the four asks for forgiveness, their soul will be forgiven and be allowed into heaven."

"Makes sense, I suppose," she said.

"If any one of the possessed dies by other means, not conducted by Minion, the prophecy is voided. And, of course, if Minion dies without completing the task, the prophecy is voided."

Grace's eyes lit up wide as if she had seen a ghost. Sheer terror filled her eyes. Her lips trembled as if she was going to cry. She thought about what the death of her brother would feel like. She couldn't think of anyone that she loved more. Losing him would be too painful to bear.

"Clearly you must see the correlation between your brother and this prophecy?"

"I do."

"And are you willing to do something about it?"

"I am willing to find my brother and make him stop this.

Even thought I know he means well, he just can't go around killing people, regardless of their crimes. That is God's job."

The Deacon smiled.

"Yes, Grace. You are perfectly right."

"I know if I find him, I can make him stop this."

"So you believe in this prophecy?"

"I'm not going that far."

The Deacon sighed.

"But will you help me find him?"

"I will. How do you plan on doing that?"

"Heading him off at the pass."

Petrified, the co-pilot could do nothing but observe the world of his afterlife. His partner, the pilot of the C130 cargo jet, had transformed from a uniformed soldier into a skinless ancient monster. The cockpit of the aircraft was now an enclosed oozing vat of oil and grease. The co-pilot couldn't even muster up the strength to scream.

From behind, a hand closed on both his eyes, escalating his panic. When the hand was removed, the horrors were gone. The cockpit returned to its normal state. The gadgets, the dials, the levers, the switches had all returned to their place. Even his pilot was back in his military fatigues and manning the aircraft as they powered ahead at thousands of feet in the sky.

"I need you to cooperate. Otherwise, you might end up somewhere less desirable," Kayden knelt down and spoke to the co-pilot very directly.

"What is this?" the co-pilot asked.

"Just shut up and help me here!" the pilot yelled at the copilot.

"We are not here to hurt you, or anyone else that would concern you. We just need a lift. Calm down and help us get there," Kayden demanded.

The copilot took a minute to examine a map.

"By now, every base in the area will know we have been

hijacked. You will never get out of our air space in one piece. They don't hesitate to shoot down aircraft anymore. Especially big ones," the co-pilot argued.

"Don't worry about that. We will be fine," Kayden firmly stated.

Back in the cargo bay, a military Hummer sat strapped in to the steel flooring of the massive craft. Inside the truck, the gang sat patiently with the windows rolled up, which cut down the jet engine noise considerably. Alton sat in the driver's seat, hammering away at his laptop. Kayden opened the driver's door.

"Keep an eye on those two. Make sure we stay on course," Kayden ordered Alton.

Alton seemed irritated, but put up no fight against the command and left the truck to see to the pilots. Kayden sat down in the driver's seat and shut the door.

"You do realize that we are marching into the jungle to find a couple of blokes that have murdered entire villages of people. They obviously have help. Most likely, they have a bloody army at their finger tips. You think you can take on an army?" Bain went on a rant in the back seat. Gar sat to his side.

"Yes I do," Kayden answered without hesitation.

"I respect that you are trying to make a change. And I'm in your corner when it comes to plucking out the weeds. But there's enough to do at home, in our neighborhoods. Why not start there? Turn things around where we live?" Gar asked.

"This matters more," Kayden answered.

Bain banged his fist against the metal door to his right. He then leaned himself forward against Kayden's seat, almost spitting in Kayden's ear as he spoke.

"I've had enough of this shit. You risk our lives, you make us into overnight fugitives, and you fly us out unguarded to who knows-the-fuck-where!" Gar grabbed Bain's shoulder to stop him from going too far. "And you are still full of secrets. I want some answers, and I want them now. Who are you?"

"Kayden Archer. Haven't we been through this enough?"

"You know what I mean!! Don't be stupid. What are you, a government agent? A military special, elite, whatever-the-hell you call yourselves?"

Kayden turned to get nose to nose with Bain. Everyone in the vehicle thought Bain had spoken his last words.

"I'm the guy that can rip you apart by just looking at you. I am the guy that can rebuild mountains if I please. I am the guy that can make you think you are being buried alive when you are actually sitting on the couch. You all are the people that are going with me. You are my other set of eyes. You are my fellow crusaders. Together, we will give this world a new face."

"Crusader? You going to tell me you are doing God's work?" Bain asked as he leaned back in his seat.

"And why not? How else would you explain a simple doctor from Philly somehow defies all known human limits overnight? How else would you explain why this all has been laid out on a clean plate? Would you call it fate? Would you call it a divine gift? Would you call it a Holy Crusade?"

Neither of the three had a response.

"I don't know what you would call me. I have no clue. I don't know why I can do these things. But the only thing that makes sense to me is that God is tired of waiting for man to grow up and live amongst each other respectfully. He is tired of mistake after mistake, sin after sin, war after war, without any lessons learned. We are designed to grow stronger after our mistakes. Yet every day, we still allow these mistakes to haunt the innocent and those that aim for progress."

"I've never been one to kneel wholeheartedly before God. If anything, I've been skeptical of the faith and theory my mother stood by unconditionally. But not anymore. Perhaps God has sent down a soldier with nothing else to lose, someone brave enough to make things right. I intend to settle my scores. After that, I am sure we will be shown the path. Fear not, we are all protected."

Kayden couldn't hear what Alton yelled in his direction as he ran out of the cockpit, but he understood it to be urgent.

102

Two jets had popped up on radar and were closing in on the C130 from behind. Kayden ordered the back cargo door opened. Kayden grabbed a strap and walked out to the very end of the ramp to overlook thousands of miles of frigid air and clouds. Within seconds, two sets of lights appeared from the clouds several miles behind at a much lower altitude.

"USS Mammoth, Big Bird fife foxtrot, bearing two-two-six, climbing to one zero, ten thousand, over," the jet pilot spoke over radio to a nearby air craft carrier.

"Roger that Big Bird, bogie is altitude two zero niner zero. Communication attempts to friendly have failed. You are to engage the target and neutralize, over," commanded the officer onboard the carrier.

"Roger that. Engaging friendly. Over."

"Tell us when you have visual, copy?"

"Roger. Big Bird will relay when have visual on bogie, over."

From Bain's point of view, it seemed as if Kayden was preparing for a jump. The wind appeared to be strong enough to pick up Kayden's body, regardless. Yet Kayden stared toward the lights as they became jets, and before long at all, the jets roared up to the C130 close enough to throw a stone to. Bain couldn't help himself to step out onto the bay door. The rest of them followed.

Before them, almost close enough to touch, the two F/A-18 fighter jets trailed the C130. Alton could not help himself and waved at the two pilots as they drove their crafts. He was slightly offended *and* worried about not receiving a return gesture of any sort.

Kayden stood with his eyes shut, concentrating on the visual image that he projected telepathically onto the two fighter pilots.

"Big Bird. Do you have a visual over?" command from the carrier asked.

"Negative Mammoth. Missile locked and ready to fire. It's as clear as day and I have no visual. Please advise, over?"

"Sniper niner-niner-bravo, do you have visual on bogie, over?" carrier asked the second F/A-18 pilot.

"That's a negative. There isn't a big green plane in two hundred miles from here, over."

"Mammoth, this is Big Bird. Isn't this where you notify us of the drill, over?"

"Big Bird, this is Mammoth. This is not a drill, over."

The co-pilot of the C130 had found his breaking point. Hallucinations, unfamiliar flight, and now there was a missile locked on his ass at point blank range. There would be no survival. And he didn't want to go out like that.

The C130 took a hard bank left when the co-pilot grabbed the wheel. Kayden, was slightly thrown off his balance, while the rest of the passengers were thrown to the floor. The jolt was enough for Kayden to lose his concentration. But only for an instant.

"Mammoth. Mammoth. I have visual, over," one F/A-18 called.

"Are you shitting me? Did this thing just get teleported?" the other F/A-18 called out, hysterically.

"Big Bird, Sniper. Engage and fire when locked, over," the carrier ordered.

One missile per jet was all it took.

One second after fire, two missiles exploded into each side of the C130. The blast immediately disabled the craft and sent it on a straight downward descent toward the ocean below. The F/A-18s, maintaining visual, followed the C130 all the way to impact. The C130 might as well have hit a solid wall. The plane shattered into several large pieces of steel when it hit the Atlantic southbound. Survival of any persons onboard would be out of the question.

"Mammoth this is Big Bird. Bogie is down in the water. I repeat. Bogie is down in the water. Do you copy position, over," the fighter pilot phoned in to base.

"Big Bird this is Mammoth. We still have bogie on our radar. Can we confirm kill, over."

"Affirmative Mammoth. Friendly bogie is down."

"Big Bird, we copy. We are still reading friendly bogie on our radar. Must be an error with our system. Let's pack it in. This mission is classified, over," was the final command from the carrier.

The two F/A-18s took a hard right and headed back to their ship. Regardless of the fact that they had fired on a friendly aircraft, this was just another completed mission for the two fighter pilots. They would fly back to their ship and brag about shooting down a C130 Super Hercules.

But their story would be untrue.

Once Gar slugged the wacked out co-pilot of the C130, the pilot used all his might to keep the giant ship in the sky. They ended up several thousand miles below their previous altitude. Kayden, minus the jolt from the plane banking, had maintained his focus. He closed his eyes and visualized the image he wanted the two F/A-18 pilots to see. He showed them two missiles hitting the plane, when in reality the two missiles shot off towards the sun. He showed them a devastated plane tumbling to the ocean in a fiery blaze, when in reality the C130 stabilized itself and was headed on its original destination.

Everyone on board was amazed. They laughed and cheered.

"Hey, you know what is awesome? We are completely off the radar. The military doesn't go looking for dead people!" Alton shouted. He high-fived Cari.

Standing firmly on the carbo bay door overlooking the ocean below, Kayden hid the smirk on his face. He didn't take his eyes away from the clouds until they landed, far away from home.

⏸

The sky was freckled with lead and the silence of the sacred lands impaired by gun shot. Donar and his men felt on edge. Usually they would hear screams following the rifle blasts. But on that day, the villagers showed no signs of fear. Collectively, the inhabitants left their homes without a fight.

Most of the villagers were mounted with pounds of jewelry, hanging from limbs and necks. Completely foreign jewelry. Rusted with age. The cracked faces and puny bodies of the elders seemed barely fit to carry such weight, yet they carried along with haste. Instead of cursing their names, the villagers kneeled at the feet of Donar and his gang of mercenaries.

Appointed guardians of the villagers, wearing fragments of old golden armor, also kneeled before their opposition, surrendering their dirty, blood-stained swords to Donar. They all gathered at the dirt road circling a temple—a massive six story, wooden, practical palace reminiscent of ancient Asian architecture.

"You have ruined us," Ospi's words to his brother Donar could barely pass for English under his thick accent. They both watched as the townspeople were being lined up in execution formation. Donar burned a cigar.

"We break here for a short while, then we march. This changes nothing. This all will be ours, just as planned." Donar replied.

"Here? No, brother. I return to where I belong, after I collect what is mine," Ospi said.

"I owe you nothing." Donar turned to his brother, looking down on him with authority.

Ospi gasped in shock. He could not respond before Donar left his side and walked to one of the surrendered guardians.

"My Lord," one of the kneeling guardians spoke to Donar upon sight, "Let my people go. Allow them to return to the caves, and we, The Marzeez—defenders of our people, will serve you honorably."

Donar looked to the so-called Marzeez. There were only six of them, and their smooth faces and perfect hands nearly led Donar to laughter. They seemed more like boys than warriors.

One of Donar's men approached the speaking guardian and pointed his assault rifle at the guardians head.

"Let me get rid of this rat, boss."

Before Donar could answer, the six guardians bounced to

their feet. At an unfathomable speed, the six guardians took positions around the threatening gunman. Each of them drove their swords into his body simultaneously. Two in his kidneys, two in his ribs, one in his heart, and one through his brain. Before the gunman fell to the ground, the Marzeez returned to their kneeling position before Donar.

The rest of Donar's men took aim at the guardians, whose surrendered swords dripped fresh blood.

"Wait!" Donar called to his men.

Donar, wide-eyed amazed, stared at each of these guardians. He let his cigar leave his lips and drop to the ground.

"You will join me if I let your people go?" Donar asked.

"It would be most gracious of you, my Lord," one of them answered.

Donar hardly took anytime at all to respond.

"Deal. Your people are free."

Ospi cursed his brother's name to the high heavens. The two trucks he intended to use to sort out the carcasses immediately drove away. Ospi limped around the villagers to a parked Jeep.

Donar blew off Ospi as if he did not exist. He looked upon his newest recruits and grinned wholeheartedly.

"Ospi, here is one for you," Donar kicked the dead body of the murdered gunman as he yelled to his brother.

Ospi had already jumped behind the wheel of the Jeep and was exiting the premises. The villagers all rose together. The younger ones assisted the elders to their feet. Without hesitation each of the villagers formed a single file line and marched toward a hillside several yards away. Many showed smiles as they marched away from the temple.

The Marzeez rose to their feet as well and carefully watched their loved ones leave their town and head straight for a cave.

Donar and his men couldn't help but watch as they funneled into the cave. Once the last villager disappeared into the dark hole, the Marzeez stood at attention in front of their new leader, Donar.

"That's where they will stay? In caves?" Donar talked down to the freed villagers.

"No, my Lord," was the answer he received from each of the Marzeez, all at once.

Donar's crew rummaged through what was left behind and each claimed quarters. Donar, along with the Marzeez, claimed the temple as his own. The Marzeez posted themselves on the perimeter, establishing a defense.

The crew couldn't resist taking a gander into the cave the villagers had disappeared into. Later, they reported to Donar what they had seen in the caves. 'There was nothing, absolutely nothing, an endless nothing.'

Donar didn't bother to investigate himself. He wasn't concerned with the villagers in the slightest. Instead, he chose to stare off the sixth level of his temple, awaiting the storm of confrontation he assumed was on its way.

Grace insisted she have the aisle seat and was adamant enough about it to stand face-to-face with a heavy, agitated lady. After a brief verbal jostle, Grace got her seat. It wasn't that she was uncomfortable looking through a window at such height, but because she was tired of looking at the world. The world and the reality of its confines had dislodged and spun in a completely different revolution. And with all the chaos that had ignited, a frantic clergyman expected Grace to pull the world back into its usual orbit.

Just hours before the flight, the authorities had detained Grace and her father for questioning. The three hours of back-and-forth provided the investigators with no new information. Neither Grace nor her father knew of Kayden's whereabouts, or his destination. To try and pry loose information that just wasn't there, the cops showed both Grace and Richard security camera footage of the courtroom that Kayden flipped upside down. At first, Grace thought she might have been watching edited video, but after several viewings, the facts became clear. Grace left the police station a changed woman. It was as if she had aged twenty years and all the playful youth had escaped her just as quickly as her assumptions of human capabilities.

Deacon James knew the white haired, clean-cut gentleman seated in the front of the cabin was an officer of the law and had an interest in Grace. But that was the least of his worries. The main concern was what exactly they should do once they landed in Belo Horizonte, Brazil, a region neither Grace nor Gregory had any useful knowledge of.

Grace looked at the paper copy of the Shudagon Prophecy as if hopelessly trying to make out the foreign literature. The end of the page intrigued her.

"The end, the ink, it's all smudged," said Grace.

"It is. I'm not sure why. It's hard to believe the document lasted long enough to make a copy."

"Where is the original?"

"Where else? The place where all the secrets are locked behind wall after wall. The place that decides what the believers believe. The Vatican."

"Looks like they spilled something at the end of the page."

"As careless as they are in the Vatican, it would not surprise me."

What did surprise Gregory was how fast the world began to set itself on fire. Only hours after Kayden's incident in downtown Philly, riots broke out sporadically in the notoriously dangerous city. Rushing to the airport, he and Grace had driven past burning cars and looting. Violence surrounded them. Gregory could only mash on the throttle, barely squeezing by the madness toward the airport.

"They are following us." Grace suggested, referring to the cop seated in the front.

"I see. My guess is that the only reason they let you on a flight is because they wanted you to lead them to your brother, which is exactly what we are doing."

"I have to. I have to get to him before they do. They will kill him."

"If they could, they already would have."

The man they suspected to be a cop left his seat to speak with the flight attendant. After the conversation, the man was allowed to use the telephone mounted on the wall used to communicate with the cock-pit.

"We don't have to aim for your brother. You know this. The prophecy clearly states that if we were to go after the last two brothers, we could end this," Gregory leaned in close to Grace from across the aisle.

"I don't care. I'm going to find my brother. "

The Deacon rubbed his temples. The last remaining "sane" ingredient of his character was fading away, but still tugged at his mind. The same ingredient that wanted to believe that the world was black and white, that there were no current instances of supernatural powers within the human race. That we are all God's creations, given free will within reasonable limits.

"Well, if anybody is going to find him, if there's anyone that can help us, it's you." Gregory said.

"Why? Why me?"

"Love. The kind that happens when you are connected by flesh and blood. Mother and daughter, father and son. Brother and sister. And up the family chain. That kind of love stays with you forever. Always connected. No disagreement or agitation can break that bond. No matter what happens. You are his sister. His only sibling."

Grace thought back to her childhood and how her older brother protected her like she was made out of glass, all the way through her high school years. Every time a boyfriend would upset her, Kayden would be the one to scold the young man before her father could. Furthermore, Kayden had always been resilient about knowing where Grace was. On Kayden's wedding night, Kayden texted Grace to ensure she made it home safely from the reception. On 9/11, the first phone call Grace received was from Kayden, ordering her to stop what she was doing and find safe shelter. Kayden never missed a birthday, graduation, piano recital, or swim match. He accepted her as a volunteer at the hospital and let her gain some hands-on experience in the medical field, in spite of his hopes for her to choose a field with less hardships.

"Regardless of his actions, he is thinking of you and his family before anyone else. I'm sure he wants nothing more than for you to live in a world without the madness, without the horrors we face every day."

Grace nodded in agreement.

"Except now he is hunting evil's most dangerous weapons. What lies ahead on his trail can turn any emotion he has into hate. Along with that hate, your brother grows more powerful than any man ever has. The combination is deadly to him and to us all. If he continues on this journey, he will let loose all the evil that exists into the world, an evil that has been locked up by God for all time. And there will be no going back. You can't fix something of that magnitude."

Expressing her bewilderment, Grace shook her head.

"I just want to wake up." Grace said.

Gregory looked at her. His eyes began to fill with tears.

"I want to know that God is watching over us, keeping us safe. Not that we have ruined God's power with our pointless war, our perversion, our disregard for life. I don't want to be known as a part of a people that have destroyed God's plan. I don't want to know that my own brother, a man that anyone can love, is now an errand boy for some evil plot."

"Like mother to child, our creator feeds off the life of his creation. It is the source of his strength. He needs it to provide the way. He needs us to remain righteous so that he may bring forth more life. And if we, his creation, stray from the path, aware or not, he will lose his grip on us, allowing evil to obtain leadership," Gregory explained.

"You sound confident, Deacon. Strong. Let me ask you, could you take a life in the name of God? Would you have the strength to do that?"

"I continue to question all that I have been told. Because of this questioning, I have acquired much knowledge of God's kingdom, which has enabled me to become a valuable resource to God. I feel his grasp. I feel his control. He is using my knowledge to save what is left of his world. No matter how trying the task is. If it is his will, it is the only way."

Grace wanted to join him by letting her tears fall, but she had already shed all of her tears. Instead she reached out and placed her hand on his shoulder to comfort him the best she could.

"He has given me strength. I intend on using it," the Deacon said.

The silver-haired, clean-cut man Grace and Gregory assumed was an officer of the law left the front of the cabin and approached the two of them. He sat down in an open seat close by.

"Hello Ms. Grace Archer, Mr. Gregory James. I am Nate Inwood of the FBI. I am afraid I have some unfortunate news for you about your brother, Kayden. He was involved in a hijacking of a military aircraft. I'm sorry to have to tell you, but this aircraft was shot down over international waters a few minutes ago. There were no survivors. I am truly sorry for your loss."

The officer returned to his seat in the front of the cabin. Grace and Gregory stared ahead, speechless for a solid hour. Part of him wanted to offer Grace his condolences. The other half was thankful it was all over. He could return home safe and back to his usual routine. The world would see this whole ordeal as a fluke and move on.

After an hour of concentrated thought, Grace smiled.

"Grace? Talk to me, Grace."

"He's alive."

This confused the priest, "What? How do you know?"

"Maybe you're right. Maybe it's because we're siblings. Maybe it's because of love. But I just know he's alive. And he's got them right where he wants them."

Sunlight poured over the tropical terrain and onto the

plateau where Donar's new kingdom sat patiently. But it wasn't the sun that woke Donar and his men on that humid morning. Round after round of artillery shot through the thick woods. Steel machinery charged through the brush, pushing over trees like twigs. Sounds of destruction came from all directions.

Donar's men rose from their beds to find their firepower missing. Every gunpowder weapon and explosive had vanished. They searched every nook of the village, but found nothing but their swords, knives, chains, and staffs, which were not particularly useful when the enemy was using artillery.

Circling along the balcony of the top floor of the temple, Donar used his binoculars to try and pinpoint the location of the ruckus, but could not see past the hills that surrounded him. For what felt like hours, Donar and his men kept their eyes on the perimeter, waiting to see what force was creating such warlike banter.

All six of the Marzeez guardians sat with their legs crossed on the north porch of the temple. They did not show signs of alarm. They did not speak to one another. They simply stared forward at nothing. The Marzeez did not respond when asked about the uproar that surrounded them.

After half an hour of gunfire and rumpus, the sounds spread to the clear sky. Donar was the first to notice tiny black dots appear from an extremely high altitude. Donar's men could hear the air being chopped by blades and looked up to see the tiny black dots become military helicopters. Donar lost count after the first three dozen aircraft appeared. In minutes, the black, heavily armed choppers descended to only a few hundred feet above the village, flying in a circular formation. Donar's men took cover while Donar inched back into the temple, still keeping an eye on the terrain around him.

The choppers had no colors or lettering to establish where they were from or what they represented. Once crouched in their personal hiding positions, Donar's men watched the black tornado of armed aircraft as they hovered above, threatening their every move.

The source of the commotion on the ground revealed itself once an infantry unit channeled into the gully. Two lines of armed soldiers in brown, unmarked uniforms marched synchronously towards the village. Donar found it odd that every member of the unknown army had the same cleanly shaven, brown-skinned face, the same height, the same assault rifle, and the same exact march. Clearly the most uniform infantry he had ever laid eyes on.

Freshly painted brown tanks appeared from a different hillside. Each one rushed down the hill in a cleanly executed attack formation toward the village. Donar's men, hiding around and under village homes, watched as the tanks lined the perimeter of the village and pointed their cannons at the guts of the temple. Still calmly seated, the Marzeez looked upon the panic of Donar's men as if they inhabited a different world all together. The impending doom that cornered their village did not distract the Marzeez in the slightest.

It wasn't long before the nameless infantry held front-line formation in front of a tank battalion. The choppers remained in their spiral overhead. Donar lit a cigar and puffed on it religiously, savoring the flavor as long as he could. There was no escape. There was nothing left to do but wait to be firebombed into the next life. Deep down, he was actually flattered by the size of the army commissioned to take his head.

Without warning, machine guns and cannons fired toward the temple as well as every village home and cottage. The Marzeez remained unresponsive, while Donar's men went for cover.

Donar did not retreat. He watched as the army pointed their weapons right at him and let the gun powder ignite. Thousands of bullets per second flooded the air. Donar stared ahead, awaiting the end.

In spite of his readiness to enter the next life, the end did not come as he expected.

Donar stood cold for a solid minute while the first attack came to a quiet close. He looked around at the temple. He saw no bullet holes, no explosions, no wreckage, and not one of his men dead or wounded. He found this humiliating.

Donar laughed. "What are you waiting for!" Donar yelled to the silent army before him.

There was no response. Donar's men crept from their hiding places, oblivious as to why they were still alive. The village should have been in pieces.

A roar projected through the air that nearly blew out Donar's eardrums. A monstrous, gritty bellow shook the Earth and cut away any bit of composure Donar's trained mercenaries had acquired.

Before they could run for the hills screaming, a colossal, winged creature flew into the center of the village, slicing through three of the choppers with its glinting, steel teeth. The choppers were cut in half and fell to the ground exploding into several pieces. The creature bore three sets of snake-skin like wings and a long, boney spine. Several asymmetrical claws hung from the creature's torso. The head of the creature was lizard-like but with an elephant's trunk ribbed with glass and rock, which it swung, destroying numerous aircrafts at a time.

More of the same breed of creatures showed up, attacking not only the aircraft but the infantry on the ground. These creatures were not hunting for food, but merely for destruction. When they weren't attacking the infantry, the flying beasts took turns diving for Donar's men, who bounced from one hiding spot to the next. Somehow, none of Donar's men could be caught by the teeth of the beasts.

From the hills, hunched-over, headless boulder giants appeared. The two legged half-rhino, half-stone creatures charged towards the tanks. Dragging along the ground, pointless limbs hung from the sides of the beasts with lifeless sloth-like fingers. The headless giants rammed the tanks with the most rounded part of their bodies. With one thrust, the tanks were ripped to pieces and stomped flat.

The remaining infantry men were ripped apart by yet another alien form. The third foreign species, a giant multilegged mantis, jumped twenty yards at a time. Atop hairy legs, black dreadlocks hung from a human female face. Her nose stretched out several meters and ended in a point. Her eyes were as black as night with a rugged and wrinkled facial complexion. With its many legs, the witch-spider tore men apart by the dozens.

Even after several attacks, none of these oddities successfully killed any of Donar's men. Either the beasts' hunting skills were poor, or the men's' evasive maneuvers had served them well.

Donar simply watched as the world he knew was flipped upside down. Both the land and the sky were flooded with beings even his sick imagination could not fabricate. He watched in awe, nearly brought to laughter at the ridiculousness that had opened up before him.

When all other retreat options failed, Donar's men bound for the temple with precise leaps, but the doors had been sealed shut. The Marzeez were no longer on the porch. A hole in a side entrance opened up to show the eyes of one of the Marzeez.

"Let us in, now!" one of Donar's soldiers demanded.

"We are to protect the Lord, not the weak of mind. We will not risk his safety because of your indolence."

"We can't fight this. Open this door!"

The roars continued, vibrating the temple. Most of Donar's men turned away from the conversation at the door to witness the horrors before them as the army was ripped apart by demons of different shapes and size—an unearthly massacre.

"Best of luck to the foolish."

The Marzeez shut the hole and left Donar's men hopeless to face a completely unfamiliar war. With shaky limbs, they stood their ground awaiting the attack by these beasts from hell. Donar kept his eyes on the show as the Marzeez joined him on the top deck. The Marzeez spread out on the top deck balcony forming a safety perimeter to protect their new leader.

Yet once the last of the advancing army was destroyed, the beasts did not approach the interior of the village. To the men's surprise, they herded out of the gully and over the hill tops to perhaps seek other targets. The flying oddities scattered and disappeared into the clouds once all the choppers had been taken out.

Donar's men did not have much time to enjoy their relief.

At the most southern hill, Donar, through his binoculars, saw a man in a ripped black shirt, combat boots, and jeans, standing tall, staring down at the village. Even from a great distance, Donar could see the rage his eyes.

Four gritty looking characters joined this proud man on the hill. At their feet, a scattered collection of assault rifles, explosives, flame throwers, and other black market weapons which had previously belonged to Donar and his men.

More men and women joined the team of five on the hill. In an instant, the hills were smothered by masses of people. At first glance, Donar saw several similarities between each lady and gent. And the closer he looked, he could not write off the fact that they appeared to be copies of one another. Of the hundreds that surrounded them, there was only the leader and replicas of a short and bald Irishman, an attractive brunette with a long blade at her side, a tall, dark rifleman behind a pair of black shades, and a skinny, nerdy youngster with a backpack. Had Donar paid attention to American news, he might have been able to put a name with each face.

The naked eyes of Donar's men couldn't pick up on the peculiar copies that surrounded them. All they saw was a more primitive army than the last two they were exposed to.

From a hillside, Kayden Archer spoke to his followers. "I believe that if you choose to follow a herd as one of the sheep, you take on the responsibility of the leadership. Although you may not lead the herd, you chose the herd. And with choices there are benefits and there are consequences. People must be responsible for their own actions. I no longer have sympathy for those that choose a vile path. So let us punish. And let us make way for those that choose their paths honorably."

The swarm of armed assailants stormed the village in an all out war-stampede. Donar's men retrieved their swords and took defensive positions, regardless of how outnumbered they were.

The clones merged together by person. A clan of six replicas of Bain approached one of Donar's men first. Each Bain wore spiked steel knuckles and charged ahead with arms wide open. Ten fists came swinging at one of Donar's men furiously. The guard defended himself with his sword, but his thrusts did not connect and his blade swung completely through his attackers as if they were of no matter and perhaps holograms. As his attacker's blows did nothing, the solider stopped his offense and stood his ground. The second he did, a solid steel knuckle shattered his jaw into pieces, spinning him around like a top. Instantly following, two steel fists collided simultaneously with his temples, turning the lights out for good. His last thoughts before his demise were geared toward deciphering which of these characters was real and which one was not. He never had a chance. And Bain immediately went fishing for other targets.

Stumbling as he ran, another of Donar's men desperately tried to dodge the shotgun fire issued by five black men coming from all directions. Shells were fired at the guard by the dozen every other second. Whatever explanation as to why he had not been hit several times from nearly point blank range, escaped him. Just when he assumed the shells were blanks, he stood tall and looked around at his attackers. A warm steel cylinder was pressed to the back of his head. He did not feel it when his brains were shot through his skull at the speed of sound and pasted onto a village home.

The mob of Cari counterparts approached three of Donar's retreating men. Each of them ducked or jumped to avoid the daggers slung in their direction. The guards were quickly cornered against a barn wall by the attacking women. Donar's men noticed a young man running towards them carrying a backpack on his shoulder, but they paid little attention once the young lady twins lashed out at them. There was no effective response, nor was there any injury from her attacks. That was until one of the twins made contact with the open armpit of one of the mercenaries, cleanly cutting his arm off at the shoulder as if his muscle tissue was made of baked cream. Blood juiced from his wound unrelentingly. Thankfully, he wouldn't feel the pain of a lost limb long. He only took a couple of panicking breaths before his head was cut from his spine and tumbled to the ground. The two remaining mercenaries watched as their co-worker was cut to pieces in a pair of masterly executed attacks.

Oddly, all the women left the two remaining men standing. All but one woman, carrying the only sword caked in blood, leaped away in giant, inhuman leaps. After feeling something attached to their backs, the guards turned to see a young man sprinting away. Alton made it away just in time before the explosives attached to the two men's bodies detonated. Along with most of the wall of a village home, body parts and fluids scattered in all directions.

The rest of Donar's men did not get the luxury of a clean death. Brutally, their lives were taken from them by four semi-professional vigilantes, backed by a false army of hallucinations.

Kayden, supplying the imagery for Donar's men, calmly walked into the village from the hillside. Once the last known target was taken down, all action in the village died. In the temple, the Marzeez had closed off every opening of the top floor to protect their new Lord.

Kayden met face to face with his crew, who had just taken out an entire team of mercenaries without breaking much of a sweat.

"That's the rest of 'em. What do you say we get out of here before we pick another fight," Bain suggested.

"What do you mean? We're not done yet. There's still the guy inside hiding like some chicken shit asshole," Alton said.

"I *mean*, let's leave him. We took out his crew. He's done. Let someone else come by and finish him off."

Kayden stared up to the top of the temple, waiting for Donar to show his face.

"He is right, we are not finished. I am not finished." Kayden stated.

"Tell us what you need." Gar made a request.

"I can take it from here." Kayden said.

The main entrance to the tower burst into thousands of shreds of wood that fell to the ground.

There was no hesitation in Kayden's stride as he walked into the temple to seek the answers for which he had traveled so far to find.

"I know what you're thinking." Deacon James stumbled on his words as he spoke to Grace at a nearly awkward proximity.

"If you knew my brother. If you really knew him, you would know he wouldn't put himself in a situation to be shot out of the sky. He's smarter than that."

"I think you could be in denial. But since we are here, I suppose we should carry on."

"Carry on? How?" Grace asked.

Deacon James gently pressed Grace on to expedite their exit from the Confins International Airport. They each carried a backpack packed with the bare necessities. The Deacon had stripped himself of his clerical garb and traveled in hiking boots and black, long-sleeve outdoor wear, regardless of the warm, tropical climate in the state of Minas Gerais in Southeastern Brazil. Grace dressed a little more comfortably in shorts and a tank top.

"In Christ's name, the prophecy can be broken. As you know, if we can convince either of the two brothers to declare Christ as their savior and beg him for his forgiveness, then all is forgotten. We can continue with the lives God has given us. That is the less violent thing to do," he explained.

"Then we should try that."

"But my guts tell me that this will not end without bloodshed."

"Why do you say that?"

"I mean, if we were able to get close enough to either of these two, we wouldn't be welcomed with open arms. Especially not long enough talk them into to devoting their lives to Christ for the survival of mankind. They will write us off as lunatics and feed us to the wolves."

"Then what else can we do, Gregory?"

The two climbed in a taxi outside of the quiet airport. The Deacon asked the driver to take them to downtown Belo Horizonte; a place with the most saturated population where they could to speak to the community in hopes of finding direction.

"I've never been one to support a holy crusade. I find that the path to salvation was set by Christ himself. Man's interpretation of his word doesn't matter when violence is put on the table. Christ never struck a man, never sent a man to fight. Rather than building an army of followers to fight, he surrendered and willingly went to the cross, fighting evil with his own bare hands."

"Right. So we do what is needed without hurting anyone."

"I wish it were that easy. God allows his design to grow and change as change may be. The results of free will can never be predicted. Sometimes we, as God's promoters, must adapt. We must contribute even more energy to his aid. We must sacrifice all to protect his grace."

"Even our innocence?"

"Yes."

Grace chuckled.

"What is funny?" the Deacon asked, slightly offended.

"I realize how crazy this all is. It's insane. This whole thing. It's a nightmare," Grace continued to force laughter, "but I think you just said that we should go on a killing spree."

"Not a killing spree, but if it's either the rest of the world or one man, then I will choose to end one life. A life that has never cared for anyone or anything but itself."

"You? You are going to kill someone?"

"If I have to, I will."

Grace chuckled again.

"You have a better plan on reserve?"

"No, I guess not." Grace gave up trying to be reasonable. She allowed her condescending tone to ring out.

Deacon James rubbed his chin and stared out of the window, agitated with his partner. The taxi reached a market place where hundreds of locals walked the streets trading their goods and services. There were children, mothers, fathers, thugs, and cons. All the mixings of a small city community.

Calmly, he continued the conversation.

"Our last resort should be obvious."

"Sorry. I didn't know there was another option."

The Deacon looked to her, surprised.

"To put a definite end to all of this, before it's too late."

Grace shrugged, not understanding the Deacon's point.

"Your brother may be special, but he is still flesh and blood. He can die, just like anyone else. If he's not dead already."

At these words, Grace seemed to pull out of her investment in this preacher instantly. She looked onto him like she would an enemy.

"Please tell me you are joking," Grace demanded.

"If your brother dies, this is all over. We win. We go home and move on."

She gaped at him with devilish eyes, hoping to intimidate him.

"It's better than the alternative!" Deacon James yelled in her face.

The taxi slowed down to a crawl. Once they stopped, Grace grabbed her pack and slung open the door to her side, nearly swiping a pedestrian. Grace leaped from the vehicle and made a dash into the busy crowd.

"Grace!"

The clergyman yelled into the crowd, hopelessly. Grace's tied up hair bounced up and down as she maneuvered quickly through the crowd, only to disappear in a matter of seconds.

Deacon James could clearly see that chasing after Grace in

this crowd would be pointless. Her fearlessness was evident and he was in no way capable of catching her. Eventually, the Deacon ordered the driver to continue.

With the rest of the world to consider, he pressed on with his crusade.

Patient steps took Kayden up to the top floor of the temple. The wood did not creak and textured rugs deadened his climb up the stairwell. There was no other movement or sound. There were no smells. Nothing to feel other than the tropical climate bringing forth his sweat.

Yet he felt eyes. He took caution, expecting an ambush.

Kayden made it to the top floor of the monastery and opened a paper-thin sliding double door to reveal a dimly-lit, open loft aligned by a balcony. Several things caught his eye, including the hand-carved statues, weapons retired on the walls, the wooden columns holding up the ceiling, and Donar Gamule standing with crossed arms, facing the hills surrounding the village. He puffed wildly at his cigar, exhibiting his arrogance. His greased back, golden hair glinted in the sunlight. Kayden couldn't see his face, but he knew it held a satisfied grin.

"Come in. Relax. Enjoy yourself. Enjoy the view." Donar called out.

"I'd rather not." Kayden replied from well across the room.

"Then go. Do as you wish."

"I will. After I've done what I came to do."

Donar chuckled with the cigar in his mouth. He turned to put his eyes on Kayden.

"My men have spoken of you."

"Before they were cut to pieces."

Donar continued to be amused.

"They told me about this magical American vigilante who cannot be touched by the law. No army can stop him. Is this you? Are you this magic man?

"Close enough."

"Tell me, Magic-Man, what is to be my fate? Are you here to kill me?"

"Yes, I believe so."

"And by killing me, you are saving the world?"

"Yes, slowly but surely."

"Tell me, using your sharpest American intellect, why do you think I do what I do?"

Kayden paused. Most of him wanted nothing more than to end the scumbag and save himself from whatever point he was about to make.

"I don't care."

"Yes you do. Because I can see that you want to rectify the situation for all the good people of the world. But the truth is, I do this because it is simple and pays well. If I didn't do this, someone else would. After I'm gone, you will be back here next week, giving another impressive show."

"No one of any value would live the life you've chosen. No one but yourself."

"You are wrong. You may know that land is difficult to take today. Because of our breeding, there is no room for us all. It is the wealthy that must control the land. Without control, they have nothing to sell and no one to buy. And the gold they are willing to sacrifice for this control would provoke even an angel to turn against his people."

"That will change."

"Funny these things you dreamers believe. If I go, there will be another in my place."

"No. I plan to put an end to both of you."

"My brother? The artist? He cannot do this work. He is only the artist."

"Then you won't mind telling me where he is."

More heavy laughter from Donar, while Kayden grew impatient.

"That is not a place you want to go. I will save you the trip."

"I will find him, either way."

"Sending you to my brother would surely mean your death. I would not mind doing so at all, but I cannot betray my own flesh and blood."

"So be it."

Kayden took one step toward Donar. The instant his boot heel hit the floor, six swordsmen dressed in golden loincloths with faces covered in golden masks appeared from the shadows. On their toes, they advanced toward Kayden with the obvious intention of defending Donar.

Caught off guard, the quickest reaction Kayden could think of was to copy himself, providing a dozen duplicates of himself that paced around the Marzeez. These illusions did halt their offensive, but they did not yield. Each of the Marzeez picked one of the targets and lashed out stylishly. All six of the Marzeez struck their targets. Six copies of Kayden went down either without certain limbs or bleeding profusely.

But the Marzeez were not fooled by Kayden's imagination. They simply eliminated all possibilities to find their true target.

Kayden kept tossing out copies of himself and backed away to get a bearing on the situation. Once he could see all of the Marzeez, he took their swords from them and slung them into the wood supports and ceiling structure. But the Marzeez did not falter, even though they were weaponless. They continued their search for him with closed fists and acrobatic foot work.

Kayden thought for sure that without their weapons, these warriors would forfeit. He was terribly wrong. In all actuality, Kayden's slight recoil was what gave him up.

With unnatural speed, one of the gold-clad soldiers sneaked up behind the real Kayden and jump-kicked him between the shoulder blades, rocking Kayden's body forward. When the soldier knew he had made actual flesh-to-flesh contact, he made a call to his affiliates. In an instant, the rest of the Marzeez left their false targets and went straight for the real Kayden. The other five Marzeez swiftly attacked Kayden with a knee to the ribs, a jab to the face, a kick to the lower back, an elbow to the ear, and lastly five sharpened fingernails across his face. Kayden went to his knees. All of the illusions disappeared.

Oddly, the Marzeez backed away. Respectfully, the Marzeez allowed Kayden to regain himself to continue the battle.

But getting to his feet took time, for Kayden was badly beaten. His ribs felt like broken glass and the cuts on this face burned as they bled. Once Kayden was on his feet, the Marzeez made their war cry loud and clear. They each went into their own unique battle stance.

Just before their attack, Kayden set up his defense. Instead of making hallucinations of himself, he made carbon copies of the Marzeez. The six Marzeez quadrupled in number in a blink of an eye. Each of them faced Kayden in a fighting formation. One after another, the false Marzeez came with swinging limbs at Kayden. The true Marzeez stood still and watched their brothers beat Kayden down. Each blow connected, tossing blood around the floor. Yet Kayden was able to stay on his feet, accepting each attack from the swarm of Marzeez.

But again, it was all a show. This time, the true Marzeez were confused enough to hesitate. And Kayden took advantage. Sneaking behind one of the Marzeez, Kayden stealthily snapped the warrior's neck with his arms. A statue of a monk left the pillar it stood against and flew into another Marzeez warrior, breaking into several pieces on impact as well as breaking open the warrior's skull to expose brain matter. The warrior fell into shock and soon perished.

This fight had never been fair, which is why Kayden abandoned his no weapon policy and retrieved two of the Marzeez's swords from the ceiling. He sent the two blades flying, twirling at shin height toward two of the Marzeez. The two warriors were so distracted, that they were not aware of the flying swords before the blades cleanly sliced through the flesh and bone of their legs. Of course the two warriors went to the ground hard, no longer having the ability to control their feet, or anything from the knee down. Blood poured from their open wounds.

All the illusions vanished at Kayden's will. The last two

remaining members of the Marzeez jerked around to face Kayden. Several ideas came to mind on how to handle the last two, but in the end, he chose the easy route.

He let half of the ceiling and temple roof fall on top of them, crushing their bodies without warning.

From the remaining top portion of the temple, Donar looked on amazed, alone, with nothing between him and the monster of a man before him. He backed himself up to the wooden balcony rails as wounded Kayden Archer marched right at him. Kayden wore pure hatred on his face. The blood that trickled from his face had mixed in with his eyes, yet he did not flinch.

Kayden reached out for Donar's throat with open hands.

Boxed in a merchant's tent, Grace found serenity among the desperate crowd of the city. Outside, she was tugged at by the arms, her hair was touched, numerous withering men made passes at her. The only place that could offer her a moment to register her situation was inside a tent full of tapestries and cheaply made jewelry, owned by a mindless owner at the end of his time.

And there was the man under the straw hat; the only white man in the herd. She had seen him at every corner. Grace considered the possibility that she was still being followed by American law enforcement. Maybe they knew Kayden is still alive? Paranoia was at an all time high.

He wore a straw farmer's hat and a dark-blue sport jacket with no shirt. His dark, tanned Dockers were the only thing keeping him from looking like a deviant flasher. The man rested most of his weight on a cane. Grace couldn't tell where his eyes were focused, but she assumed they were on her.

Yet, even with the gentleman's odd appearance, she did not completely fear him; rather, it made her somewhat hopeful that there was another person that possibly spoke her language.

The tent owner, who was perhaps a hundred years old, did not even notice Grace standing in his store. He sat in a camping chair slighting shaking with his eyes fixed on the traffic outside. Grace could have stayed there for hours if the old man hadn't started chanting some unintelligible ramble, frightening Grace out of the tent and back into the crowd.

She was immediately accosted by several merchants offering crafts and jewelry. She ran, weaving through the locals without a clue of where she would end up.

A cane suddenly appeared in her path, nearly tripping her.

"Lost? You look lost?" a raspy voice carried by an Eastern European accent asked Grace.

Grace looked up to see that the odd gentleman she had notice earlier had somehow appeared right before her. She couldn't find the words to make an intelligent reply.

"Young girl. What are you here for?" asked the man under the straw hat. The English language did not suit him, but the accent was far different than that of the Brazilians.

Grace had no choice but to try and escape of her predicament, even if it meant communicating with a strange man.

"Please sir. I need help."

"Of course. Tell me the matter young lady?"

"I came here to look for my brother. I have to find him. He is supposed to be somewhere close."

"I see. Friends come and friends go, but the sibling....they will never leave."

Grace nodded. The man looked around at his perimeter as if he was hoping to stay unnoticed by everyone except for Grace.

"Are you American?"

"Yes," Grace answered.

"And why is your American brother in Brazil?"

"I'm not even sure he is. Maybe, he is looking for someone. I don't know."

"Looking for someone?"

"Yes. It's complicated."

"I see. Complicated. Well, we travel to consulate. There, your Americans may help your quest.

"Maybe I just need to go back home."

"I have vehicle close by. Come."

"No thanks, I will just take a cab."

"Cab? Very well. Take much care. Danger everywhere in these people."

Grace waved at a cab that approached the two of them. The small compact car stopped right at her feet. The driver signaled her to step inside.

"Maybe I escort you? Ensure your safety?" the man under the straw hat suggested.

Grace did not argue and jumped in the cab. Her escort followed.

"Airport?" her escort asked.

Grace nodded. He then spoke to the cab driver in Portuguese. The cab immediately raced off into the busy streets.

"You are very lucky girl. People here would see you as commodity. Some would take you as their property. You are very lucky."

"I don't know what I'm doing anymore. It's all so confusing," Grace explained.

"I see. Youth is full of confusion. Many professors teaching different stories, ideas; it is difficult to tell true from false."

"What did you say your name was?" Grace spoke as politely as she could, looking down at the floor board.

"Ospi. It is the name of my grandfather."

The moment Ospi answered Grace, she felt a prick at the back of her neck. She saw Ospi's hand come from behind her seat and to his straw hat. As soon as he pulled it off his bald head and threw it on the floorboard, she recognized his features.

Ospi Gamule—not only had she seen him on the news, but Deacon James had pulled up numerous pictures and articles on the man. This was the man her brother hunted at that very moment. If Grace had found the strength to destroy Ospi, the prophecy the Deacon spoke of would be instantly voided.

But her strength left her. Her mind went foggy and she couldn't control her limbs. Her arms were the first thing to go limp. She lost feeling in her legs. Her eyelids acted like anchors. Her spine couldn't seem to support her head.

"Sleep now, young one. A new home awaits."

When the cab halted at a stoplight, Ospi reached for the driver. With almost military trained precision, Ospi snapped the cab driver's neck. He then got out of the vehicle, pushed the driver over to the passenger seat, got behind the wheel, and drove the cab in the opposite direction.

Grace drifted in and out of consciousness during the next hour before completely passing out. During that time, she felt the cab bouncing through rough terrain. She felt her body being carried, followed by a chilling cold. The last thing she heard before her deep sleep was screaming.

Kayden let just enough pressure off of Donar's throat to allow him to speak.

"I've beaten you. You are finished." Kayden spoke as he held Donar so close that their eyes nearly touched.

Kayden was hoping to strike fear into Donar, Donar only laughed; weakened, careless laughter.

"Tell me where he is."

"Fool!"

"Tell me!"

"No," Donar laughed in Kayden's bleeding face.

Kayden rammed his own forehead into Donar's nose, shattering the cartilage inside. Blood shot from Donar's nostrils. Kayden didn't stop there and landed several haymaker punches to Donar's cheekbones.

But even with the injuries he sustained, Donar still managed to taunt Kayden with laughter.

"You Americans. You think by bullying the rest of the world that you can get your way. The rest of us have been fighting for thousands of years. You don't scare me. You have not shown me anything that hasn't been done before."

The remaining statues shook and fell to the floor. The half

of the roof that was still attached began to crumble apart, as if they had been hit with an earthquake. Underneath Kayden and Donar, a jagged, wooden square broke apart from the rest of the floor. The floor freed itself from the structure and separated the two men from the rest of the temple.

This square slab began to rise with the two men standing on it. Gradually, they floated upwards, rising directly above the temple. Kayden continued to squeeze Donar's throat, staring into his soul with eyes poisoned with hate. In seconds, Kayden and Donar were a hundred feet in the air. Bain and the crew watched from below in awe.

"Know this. I will wipe the Earth of those like you. Those who profit from human loss and suffering. Those who treat people's lives like stock. Those who can never have enough!" Kayden preached to Donar.

Donar looked around to see the world far below him. He smiled as if he had finally lost his sanity altogether.

"I was wrong. You have been hiding your good tricks." Donar said, and carried on his laughter. "Brother is going to love your company."

"Where is he?"

"Don't you worry. You will find him. His door will be open. I only wish I could be there. Glorious!"

"Where is he?"

"Deep below."

Donar laughed some more.

"Tell me!"

"His lives in hell."

Kayden stopped his angry yelling. He slowly let go of Donar.

Once out of Kayden's grasp, Donar fell backwards and off the hovering plank of wood. His body tumbled over twice. To his end, Donar came into contact with several of the remaining structural beams of the temple, crashing through to the bottom floor.

Kayden gently floated back down to the surface by way of the jagged slab of wood.

On the ground, Bain and the crew waited patiently for their leader's next call.

"Your face? What happened?" Bain asked Kayden.

But Kayden ignored the question. With his feet on the ground, Kayden walked over to Gar. At gunpoint, Gar secured the last remaining member of Donar's team. The dusty mercenary's hands were bound behind his back, blood dripped from his busted lip.

"Well done," Kayden thanked Gar for keeping someone alive to talk.

"You got it. He says he knows where the brother lives. Some cave about an hour from here," Gar replied.

"Then he will take us."

"Whatever we do, we should do it now. I'm sure if we found this place, others will too." Bain suggested.

Kayden nodded and was then suddenly reminded of his injuries with a sharp pain to his ribs. He bent over, staggering in his stride. The others didn't know how to react. Kayden was a God in their eyes and they hadn't the slightest idea of how to aid a God.

Kayden stumbled over to a wooden hand rail that guarded a stairwell to the temple. There, he gained his balance while attempting to grasp his pain, grinding his teeth to force the anguish free from his chest.

In that moment, he questioned himself. Even with marvelous abilities, Kayden would always be a mortal man. Death would continue to chase him. And in the last hour, he had come closer to losing the battle of life than ever before.

He gripped the handrail, praying that somehow he could transfer his pain to the handrail that he leaned upon.

All doubt left when his silent prayers were fulfilled. The wooden rail in his grasp began to blacken like grilling coals. Then the wood began to smoke. And only seconds after his prayer, a flame engulfed the handrail.

But Kayden did not let go. He looked up to see the wood on fire with his hand in the midst of the flame. He pulled his hand away quickly. Expecting to see boiling skin, he was amazed to find his hand without a single burn wound.

The wooded railing stayed ablaze and started to crumble apart into several pieces. Sweltering, the heat given off by the isolated flame stunned them all. Kayden, along with his crew, watched in astonishment at yet another nightmarish occurrence unfolded before their eyes.

In an attempt to control the oddity, Kayden placed his hand on another section of the guard rail. Nothing happened. He squeezed the rail slightly. Again, nothing. But when he shut his eyes and tried to flush out all the pain, the guilt, the torment from his guts, the wood immediately ignited, creating a much more powerful blaze. The fire spread faster than anyone could have anticipated. In seconds, the entire lower half of the temple was completely on fire and spreading quickly.

The crew stepped back, worried that the building would tumble down on their heads.

Kayden only took a couple of gentle steps back. After a few minutes, Kayden saw a towering inferno before him. The fire was hot enough to singe eyebrows and force sweat from pores. Everyone but Kayden stepped away from perimeter of the burning building.

Instead of retreating, Kayden concentrated on the building. He focused all his rage, all his hate, all his pain on the center of the fire.

With a sudden growl, the building broke into millions of burning splinters, projecting away from Kayden as if he released a fireball, destroying any remembrance of the temple.

The hearts of Bain, Alton, Gar, and Cari all dropped to their bellies as they witnessed Kayden's third and most destructive gift – the ability to create fire. Standing with his followers in a foreign jungle, he had physical control over anything in his path. His thoughts were projected into reality for everyone to see. And after his encounter with Donar Gamule, he could burn away anything he wished.

There was no limit to what he could do to the world.

If Deacon Gregory James had ever possessed any patience, he had lost it under the Brazilian sun, where it would have been the most useful. Liberdade Avenue was the hub for all those who chose to live without restraints: drug users, abusers, and dealers; thieves, hit men, money launderers, and gamblers. Each inhabitant of the street picked a divvy pub and used it as an office, and like any office, if you didn't have an appointment, you were not welcome. No one bothered to explain the rules to the Deacon.

The preacher, out of uniform, questioned every man, woman, and child that crossed his path from the moment he got out of the taxi. Few spoke English. He willingly gave what money he had in exchange for information. Unsurprisingly, all of the information he was given only led him in circles. The one good piece of advice he was given included no charge – get off of Liberdade Avenue and never come back. He ignored such council.

Out of breath, but still eager, Deacon James marched into Imo's den, a greasy spot with an oscillating fan and an ice chest. The bar, which was the only maintained furnishing in Imo's den, was claimed by three men and a sweaty bartender. Leaning against the shiny bar, a well-fed gentleman wearing a gun-holster stared at the Deacon. The pistol in his holster glistened like the oily, lengthy pony-tail that had grown all the way to his ass. Wearing a cheap blazer, the man that stood next to him shared the same security personnel look. Deacon James instantly assumed they were protecting the seated elderly gentleman, mashing the buttons on his blackberry while reading a newspaper. He wore sunglasses and had numerous rings on his wrinkled fingers. His black hair was graying and his hands slightly twitched.

"Does anyone speak English?" the Deacon yelled wildly in between his panting breaths. The gunman with the pony tail put his hand on his pistol, and pointed his other at the door.

"Nothing in here for you old man," the gunman spoke.

But hearing something intelligible only spiked the Deacon's interest.

"Please, I need help. I need to find someone."

"Did you not hear? This place is not for you. Go back to where you came from."

"This is more important that you or I. I'm looking for two brothers. The Gamule brothers. I know they have been in the—"

Looking up from his blackberry, the gentleman at the bar interrupted the Deacon.

"Gamule. And what business does a man like you have with the Gamule brothers?"

"You know them?"

"Not personally, no. I stay away from those surrounded by hatred."

"If I don't find them, it could mean the end of the world. Please tell me."

The three men laughed at the clergyman.

"Those two Russian idiots are dead by now. You won't find them."

"Please, I have to try."

"A death wish I see?"

"A mission from God."

The room fell silent. The two security agents looked to their employer for the next call.

"Take this madman to that Russian's cave. Let him seal his own fate."

It took Grace several slow, intoxicated moments to figure out that her eyelids were open and she wasn't experiencing some drug-induced blackout. She batted her eyes, but only darkness remained. If not for the faint reflection bouncing off a far away crevice, she would not have been afforded sight. The ground which she laid upon was not flat, but had an odd shape and feel. Her head lay on a solid, cold section but the rest of her lay upon a soft, spongy indention. The chemical smell was somewhat familiar to her; a sharp scent similar to hospital aroma.

As Grace gradually regained consciousness, she could feel that her hands were bound to a pole that protruded from the ground. The thin substance that was tied around her wrists nearly cut off all the blood that flowed to her fingertips. She would have been satisfied to roll over from lying on her side to lying on her back, but with her hands tied up to the pole, she could not maneuver.

Her first cry out into the darkness was more of a moan than a cry for help. The drug that had temporarily taken away her reality had also inhibited all of her basic functions. Drool ran down her check and neck.

The tiny fracture of light that vaguely showed Grace her surroundings flickered and indicated to her slowly gathering thought process that there was a fire close by—that and the soft crackling that became more audible as she came to.

"Help!" Grace bellowed out just as soon as she regained total feeling in her tongue and cheeks.

She received an instantaneous, yet undesirable reply. Instead of someone finding her voice, freeing her from her constraints, and guiding her out of the dark hole she laid in, the response to her plea was only more pleas. Cries for help. Cries of torment and anguish. Cries of desperation. Grace's call for help was answered by an orchestra of pain. Although, their voices were far more fraught than Grace's could ever be. Men, women, and children from all corners of her perception demanded that Grace relieve them of their torment.

The orange flickering glow that barely crept in gave Grace the hint that she wasn't the only one imprisoned. In the faint splashes of light, she saw faces and hunched over bodies, some of which were bound to three-foot protrusions in the shape of leg bones. Out of the many prisoners, some seemed very alive and some did not.

After hearing the wall of cries, she immediately felt guilty for even asking for help. From what she could gather, she didn't have it half as bad as those surrounding her in the darkness. She was merely a new addition. To show what little respect she could, Grace kept her weeping to a minimum.

Grace was jolted by a distinct scream of pain that no performance could ever repeat accurately. Just as the scream projected off the surfaces of Grace's surroundings, the light grew in intensity. She could actually make out the dome-like natural structure of the cave she lay in. The surface of the fabricated walls was highly textured with little repetition in the design. Knots, protrusions, moldings were scattered across the surface abstractly.

When the ground became visible, she could see that the hard, partially rounded object that Grace was forced to lay her head on was a fragment of a human skull. Several bone fragments made up the ground floor along with other unknown materials.

It looked organic. It almost felt alive.

Grace frantically tried to push herself free with her legs, but it was no use. During all the kicking, her feet landed in a pool of thick liquid, soaking her shoe and sock.

She wanted to hold in her screams, but instead she joined in, praying loud enough to hear herself over the bellows around her. She begged for the heavens to put her back to sleep.

But it wasn't the heavens that took her. Hard, metallic footsteps broke through the moans. Crippled footsteps against the half-spongy, half-solid ground that came straight for her. Cold hands seized Grace by the shoulders.

As she was cut loose and dragged through the dark, her feet bumped into several crouched bodies. Starved mouths tried to bite into her legs as she was pulled through. Her own screams were masked by those around her. The others cried to whoever was shuttling her. They wanted to leave, regardless of where it took them. The voices cursed Grace for being chosen.

Before she fainted, she felt increasing warmth, much like fire. But before she could see where she had been relocated, she thankfully lost consciousness, escaping from the madness into nothingness.

⏸

"There is no fucking way!" Alton declared.

"This idiot wants us to walk into a death trap!" Bain yelled.

Kayden, only a few strides from entering the dark, narrow hole, listened to Bain and Alton's rant, but did not pay full attention to their defense. The last of Donar's men had led them to this hole. Of to the side, the detained mercenary unwillingly kneeled with his knees dug deep into a the mud. Just outside of the cave entrance, the terrain was chewed up by truck tires. Despite its location far off the beaten path, the entrance to the cave had seen plenty of traffic.

"Can't you just blow this whole thing up or something? Save us time. Then we can go home. Right?" Alton continued.

"No. Not this time." Kayden answered.

"Well enjoy yourself mate. We will be here waiting for you."

"Are you afraid of the dark?" Kayden asked Bain.

"Oh, you are the scholar. A man on his fucking knees just told you what goes in there," Bain pointed to the mercenary. "People, mate. People go down in there. People not like you, but like me and the rest of us. And you know what doesn't come out of there, mate? People! So tell me, kind sir, why the fuck would I want to go in somewhere where the odds tell me that I won't be coming out?"

"Because you are with me."

"What is so damn special about this evil son-of-a-bitch?" Alton asked.

"He's a mass murderer. He ends innocent life for profit.

138

We have the chance to stop him for good. Would you call that special?"

Gar and Cari looked at each other, silently deciding who to agree with.

"Then we go. Finish this job. Then move on to the next. Like we always do." Gar added.

Alton stomped off, infuriated. But he didn't go far. All four of them knew they had made a commitment, formal or not. They had a future with Kayden. Turning their backs on something this unique and powerful would be no different than turning their backs on God.

"What do you want to do with him?" Cari asked, pointing her long blade towards their prisoner.

"Leave him tied up here," Kayden ordered.

Gar pulled out a flashlight from their jeep. Kayden took a look at the light in Gar's hand and frowned. The flashlight was ripped away from Gar and flung off into the wilderness. In the same moment, a bulky tree branch broke away from the closest tree. Upon impact with the ground beneath, the branch split and dozens of fragments scattered within a ten foot diameter. Kayden, manipulating nature once again, walked into the scattered lot and picked up five slender branches. He then passed them out to his followers.

They were all unsure of the purpose of the wood until they were smothered in total darkness only fifty paces into the narrow tunnel of the cave. With only a touch from his fingers, Kayden lit the ends of each stick of wood with enough flame to light their footsteps. Once he had a spark, he could control the intensity of each flame using only a little concentration. The sticks burned slowly, but effectively.

Kayden led the way. At the tail of the line, Bain closely followed the others at a comfortable distance. If their adrenaline hadn't been pumping full tilt, they would have noticed the gradual drop in temperature as they proceeded. What weapons they had were drawn and cocked, and their shaky fingers rested on the triggers. If as much as a rat showed its dirty face, it wouldn't have survived an introduction.

The first noticeable artifact was an archway that rose close to twenty feet high and stretched near thirty feet from one end of the cave to the next, just as the narrow tunnel opened into a wide arena.

"Looks way too fancy for a dirty cave. The detail, it's incredible." Cari pointed out the unique design of the archway and the abstract pattern of the supporting structure.

Bain nearly let the bullets fly when he came upon a statue standing alone. At first sight, Bain had mistaken it for a person.

"Boss, look." Gar pointed the barrel of his shotgun at wall sconce made of straw and twine. Other sconces came into view. Their appeared to be several aligning the circular perimeter around them.

Bain, Cari, and Alton walked right up to the statue, just as Kayden lit all the torches. They jumped back away from the statue, horrified of what they saw.

A chalky white statue of an angel stood. There was no head atop the angel's neck. Instead, the angel stuck out both open hands holding its own head as if to offer it to them. The detail of the body led them to believe it was a wax sculpture or an expert clay model. The wings attached were red and fleshy, like fresh meat pulled apart. No symmetry in the shredded wings was implemented in the design.

"What is this place?" Alton quivered and considered retreat.

"It's just a garden statue." Kayden did what he could to keep everyone calm.

With both hands, Cari felt the head the angel held. She described the texture as leathery. The lips felt like a sponge. Hanging from the head were golden strands of well conditioned hair that fluttered in the faint breeze. Every detail seemed studied. Yet, no one was sure why.

While Cari inspected the angel, Bain got a closer look at the walls. A thick sheet of material had been stretched from top to bottom to create an enclosure around the dome. Within the walls, the only visible part of the natural rock was above. On the ground, more slabs of the thick material were laid flat and included random indentions to form abstract patterns.

Six separate entrances were revealed by the sconce light. Only darkness continued past the openings.

"These walls, they feel like rubber or plastic even." Bain offered as he inspected the surfaces surrounding him.

"Let's split up." Kayden suggested.

His desperation to find this man had peaked. Caves, statues, strange walls, torches—nothing seemed to grab his attention in the slightest way. Nothing seemed to rattle him. The others were nearly paralyzed by whatever nightmare they had entered into.

"Have you lost all your fucking sense?" Bain asked.

"The quicker we finish this, the quicker we can leave." Kayden replied.

"Who knows what's behind those doors."

"We are armed!" Kayden responded with anger.

"You are armed, mate! We have a couple of guns and our heads. You have a whole mess of weapons at your disposal. We stay with you." Bain stood his ground.

"Still afraid of the dark, I see." Kayden tried insult.

Bain stepped to Kayden to offer every bit of his guts to oppose him.

"I am one breath away from putting a couple of bullets in your legs and leaving you here to die." Bain said, but Kayden could see right through him. An empty threat, but provoked. "This place is not right. And after that beating you just took, I don't think you're in the shape to be rummaging around in a dark cave."

"I'm fine."

"Bullshit." Alton piped in.

"No you're not, mate. You are far from it. For reasons unknown to us, you are angry with this old man. You have something personal against this fucker, you're just not telling us why. I am all for crushing the life out of thousands of twisted, fucking scum, but I'm not for walking straight into an ambush."

"Maybe you should go. If you are too scared to face an old, crippled man, then maybe you should just go back home."

Kayden tested Bain's wits as well as his courage with his soft-spoken words. Bain frowned at him. He was pissed to no good end.

"Maybe you should all just go home." Kayden spoke louder to them all.

They all kept quiet for a few seconds as they considered their possibilities.

"We are with you boss." Gar spoke up, again driving them forward.

"Good, pick a door. Yell if you find the old man."

Kayden marched forward into one of the five entrances with a torch in his hand. The rest grabbed a lit torch as well and each picked a room. Each of them, even Kayden, crept forward through narrow, silent passageways one foot at a time, their heads on a swivel and their eyes wide open.

Never before had Deacon James endured car sickness, but the jerky, unstable race along the barely beaten paths through the jungle hills, cornering cliff edges at thirty miles per hour, nearly made him woozy enough to add his breakfast to floor of the four-wheel drive truck. The driver couldn't sit still, and he was constantly scanning the area around him as he piloted the topless truck through the terrain.

"Can you slow down, please!" the Deacon asked the driver for the fifth time.

The driver did not respond to the Deacon's concerns, and maintained a reckless pace with wide-open eyes.

The truck hopped a bump and splashed hard into a puddle of rainwater. When the vehicle came to a stop, the driver began yelling frantically, waving his hand to shoo off Deacon James from the vehicle.

"Where am I going?" the Deacon asked.

The only response he was given was more unintelligible yelling and a pointed finger towards a hill off in the distance where another vehicle sat. Gregory jumped out of the truck. Once his feet hit the ground, the truck's engine roared. The driver did a quick u-turn and disappeared in seconds.

The Deacon trekked through the mud toward the parked vehicle. A figure came in view. A man sat in the dirt with his hands bound behind his back. The Deacon assumed the man was dead until he awoke the stranger with a nudge. His first instinct was to free the man from his restraints, but he hesitated.

"Who are you?" the Deacon asked.

"I'm retired. Forever."

"Why were you tied up? And where are we?"

"Somewhere you don't want to be. These freaks tied me up here after they killed all of my men and my chief. I think they drugged us. The shit I saw, you wouldn't believe."

"Do you know who they were?"

"Group of hard asses. And one evil son-of-a-bitch. I've never seen anything like it."

"Where did they go?"

"Down there."

Donar's last man pointed to the cave.

"What's down there?"

"I haven't the slightest. An old cripple lives there. All I know is that anyone I've ever seen go in there, dead or alive, never comes back out."

"Donar Gamule? Is he down there?"

The dirty soldier was stunned. "How do you know that name? Who are you?"

"Just answer me son, please. Donar Gamule. Do you know who he is?"

"He's my chief. Was my chief. They killed him. Dropped him from the sky. He's gone."

"Who killed him?"

"A madman. A wizard or something. He can do these things. Make you see people that are not really there. Set fires with his eyes. Maybe I'm just losing my shit."

Deacon James let his head hang. The hope that he could stop this madness from happening disappeared with the explanation the young soldier offered.

"Son, please tell me, is this old crippled man you speak of Donar's brother?"

"Don't have a clue. No one does. He's just this weird old guy that collects all the prisoners *and* the bodies."

Deacon James released the solider from his bindings and headed towards the cave with a strong foot.

"If you go down there, you won't come back."

Deacon James turned to face the young soldier. He collected his thoughts and said what he considered to be his last words.

"If I don't, we all perish. May God give me the strength I need to carry on. I do this in His name."

The soldier shrugged, confused. The Deacon turned and marched into the tunnel with nothing but a flashlight.

⑪

In all the days of his young life, Alton Harper had never witnessed art in its most vile form until he left the narrow passage way and entered an open chamber that, for all practical purposes, was an art exhibit. Shameful, he thought, that he was forced to admire alone.

The chamber was a replica of a Roman bathhouse. Pillars held the structure in place. Actual baths were carved into the marble ground. Steam moistened the air. The room authentically represented the Roman era with a delicacy unmatched by any painting or film that Alton had ever seen.

But it wasn't the structure that completed the realism of the piece. It wasn't the baths, the tile, the steam, or the pillars. Mannequins filled the room, posing in casual stature, mid-conversation, enjoying their baths. Some naked or half-naked men stood in corners conversing. Some lay in baths, or closely watched others bathe. Some embraced while bathing. All of them seemed joyful and accepted one another closely as comrades, like men of power rejoicing their achievements and basking in the fruits of success.

Alton could not keep himself from closely examining the mannequins one by one. The texture of their bodies made any wax museum or national monument seem amateur. Alton felt as if he was touching true human skin as he laid his hands on them. Their teeth, their eyes, their nails, their tongues, all seemed as real as Alton himself. Their attire was exactly what Alton expected; fine linens and thick golden jewelry.

If Alton had taken a photo, it would have been easy to believe that Alton had traveled through time to capture the shot. Everything was pure, excellently crafted, and excellently executed; all except for the bath water.

Blood, of the thickest consistency, mildly bubbled in the baths. Several mannequins enjoyed their dip into the dark red. It dripped down their fingers and was blotted on their necks and faces.

At the opposite end of the cave, Cari marveled at another finely tuned exhibit. The one she had stumbled into represented an urban animal fight set in a 21st century gambling ring. Fake men and women gathered around a circular wire cage. They each seemed to be yelling and screaming in their frozen stance. Many held cash in their outreached hands. They all stood in front of walls covered in graffiti, crumbling with age.

Cari slowly moved toward the cage to be able to see what beasts were inside.

But they were not beasts. They did not have four legs, they were not covered in hair, they did not have sharp teeth. These were people. Two women were on their hands and knees, clawing at each other. Hair hung tangled about their faces. Grime and filth covered their hideously thin bodies. Their bones stuck out of their flesh and their eyes seemed to sink into their skulls. With these mannequins, the fabrication method was visible, for the stitches that ran across their bodies were intentionally visible. It appeared to Cari that several different types of material were used to form their figures. Dark skin, pale skin, tan skin, an assortment of skin-like material was patched together to form their outer layer.

Cari jumped back after she thought she saw one of the figures blink.

Kayden nearly dug his dingy fingernails in his own paws, fighting through his hunger to catch the hunted. He knew all too well that he could turn this place upside down. Just one thought, and the walls would crumble. The fleshy material that made up the walls would melt with just a touch, leaving his prey nowhere to hide.

He had left his loved ones to be in a demented cave, causing a national panic while leading his followers into a grim uncertainty. All for a glimpse and a brief conversation. Very brief.

Kayden thought of himself as a forced guest, imposing on the old man's turf, studying his lifestyle before the kill. He had to know. He had to find him. He had to look him in the eye.

As he walked through the narrow tunnel, he thought of the countless opportunities at every corner of the Earth to use his abilities for the good of the people. End wars, build structures, provide safe environments for those living in fear. He could do anything. Be anything. Perhaps spend a little time enjoying the gifts he had received. A God, they would call him. A savior. With only a little effort, he could make peace throughout the world.

But he was here, deep in the Earth's crust, only for his personal satisfaction. He knew without his brother, Ospi Gamule's days of killing were over. Before long, some authority would come along, dig the old man out, throw him behind bars, or maybe even execute him right on the spot.

Just a little more time, he thought. After this was over, he swore to himself that he would make the world a better place.

Kayden had found himself in a narrow passageway lit by more sconces hanging on the walls. Several symmetrical crevices were carved into the stone walls. Inside the crevices were severed human heads of all ethnicities; each one frozen in time with an expression of panic, horror, distress, or discomfort.

Kayden's march had slowed to a hesitant stride. Even the magical vigilante could not ignore his own fear.

"I know of you."

A hollow voice spoke. The source of the omnipresent voice was impossible to pinpoint. Kayden only heard bouncing echoes from all directions.

"You have caused a great panic in the red, white, and blue. You have fooled the Americans into believing you are a god."

The Russian voice continued. It had an aged tone, possibly from a man nearing old age.

"Where are you?" Kayden tried to speak back as he passed a face that had decayed on one side, while the other looked alive and well. It was the face of an Asian teenage boy.

"Why are you here?" asked the voice.

"To put an end to this," Kayden answered.

"Is that so? I am honored."

"Can we speak face to face?"

"I think not. If what they say is true, I am no match for a god."

Kayden passed another face, this one an elderly woman. The realism took him for a spin. Each wrinkle, each blemish had been maintained. It would not have been much of a surprise to hear the face speak.

"Your brother had the guts to face me, before I killed him." Kayden struck.

There was silence. Kayden smiled. He knew he had landed a blow to this monster's heart.

"His time was long overdue. Perhaps we will be allies once again in the afterlife. It was a glorious crusade."

"A couple of vultures terrorizing the innocent while they sleep in their beds. Cowards!"

Laughter from all corners.

"Cowards? I think you give us too much credit. We are merely the courier for the throne. It is those with power that you seek. They pave over the weak like dirt, yet they protect us."

"And look at me. In your home. Untouched."

"You have found us because of our own negligence. The throne has abandoned us because of our greed. Rightfully so. Rightfully so."

Metallic steps resonated through the passageway and rapidly faded away in seconds.

"Show yourself!"

Kayden heard no reply.

A sharp, emotional pain struck Kayden in the chest. He nearly cried. It hurt to hear that voice. So sinister, so horrific, but it was the comfort he found in the voice that hurt. He wanted more. He needed more. He would take all he could before it stopped forever.

War. A permitted accumulation of violence. One catastrophe after another. A cryptic agenda forced into action by leaders seated at a comfortable distance.

Gar had found his way into an arena. Inside, a complete exhibit replicating instances of battle, derived from several different conflicts including Vietnam, Medieval European wars, Roman wars, the Civil War, and the Middle Eastern conflicts were all lumped together in a frozen every-man-for-himself brawl. Some carried swords, some carried guns, cannons, or explosives. Hundreds of soldiers killed themselves to be the last man standing. There were no sides, there was no base, and there was no shelter. Only the fight.

As he walked through, Gar kept his weapon, waiting for any one of the blood lusting statues to take a poke at him.

Flawlessly executed, the instant of a bomb detonation was

included in the piece. Bodies and body parts were projected from the source of the explosion and hung by fishing wire from the ceiling to accurately portray that instant in time.

At one corner, a medieval, axe-toting warrior manned a machine gun mounted on an army truck, ready to fire on all in his path.

Men clawed at each other with their dull finger nails. Some men fought with their teeth. Throats were slit, limbs hacked off, and eyes gouged out. Yet, their wounds wouldn't stop them.

Gar rounded a patch where men trampled over one another to reach a flag. He stopped and looked up, pointing his weapon.

In elevated seating platforms, there were frozen onlookers watching the fight with a silent and motionless glare. There were kings, politicians, wives, and business men all seated and passionately watching the war from above. They celebrated, pointing and laughing, cheering and taunting.

The onlookers had more impact on Gar than the chaos on the ground. He had seen war after war. It was home. But there was something about having the pushers-of-the-button within sight that really brought the hate. He had spent his life in the muck, never really knowing what the real motive was to take the life of an enemy. There was a time when he trusted his leaders, regardless of how many times he felt misled.

Two words came to thought: never again.

He continued to circle though the arena, paying his respects to the fight.

At first, the heads of the hall disturbed Kayden, but after miles of walking, they became more irritating than anything else. After what felt like an hour of marching, the actual length of the passageway became more impressive than its decor.

"How do you favor the work?" the hiding voice spoke again to Kayden.

"I'm failing to see the point in all of this." Kayden answered.

"There is no point. It's only a mirror. A reflection of yourself."

"Right. And how long have you been polishing this mirror?"

"All my life."

"You spent your entire life making paper dolls in a cave? Interesting decision."

More intense laughter.

"Made this out of paper? You must be joking." the voice asked.

"Or clay, or mud, or plaster."

"You are no god. A god would be far more attentive."

"Oh, enlighten me, artist. What is your secret ingredient?"

"My brother and I had quite a unique arrangement. It truly was an efficient instrument of natural beauty. Men with gold would employ Donar to rid them of the peasants and villagers that horded the lands. The initial challenge should be obvious. Where to put the carcasses so they can never be found?"

Kayden set aside his irritation to digest the explanation. This made him halt his stride and look to one of the lifeless heads.

"As a young artist, I bled to find my true expression. My disability was always an obstacle, but as my mind progressed, it became my inspiration. Flesh. Transformed. Reprocessed. Reborn."

More laughter from the man that hid.

Kayden reached out to touch one of the faces. He was horrified by the texture. It felt like real flesh.

"And I shall dedicate my final work to you, my Godlike visitor."

The metallic steps continued until they disappeared.

Grasping the situation was difficult for Kayden. Never once had he considered such a horrid idea, but as he gazed around the hall, the reality became crystal clear. It was human flesh he was looking upon. Dead flesh, but regardless, these heads had once been attached to bodies. They had breathed, thought, laughed, and cried. And the left over innards of dead victims were stitched together to make the walls that directed him.

Yet again, Kayden's standard for the actions of evil had reached a new pinnacle. He had been introduced to a new category of sin. It was a sin that no book of law, no international guideline, no constitution, or no holy book had set a rule for. No one in their right mind could predict something of this magnitude, much less prepare for it.

To see how art could have evolved into creating exhibits out of human flesh broke Kayden's confidence. He knew it could only get worse. In this life, there would always be one catastrophe after another, one extreme followed by the next. New ways of destroying man popped up like new smartphones, each one finding a way to outsmart the next.

With his head down and the whites of his eyes glowing, Kayden pressed on in search of the end of this derangement, listening carefully to the air above for the voice to speak again. He silently vowed to make sure it was the last of the conversations with the madden artist.

Like many in the same situation, Bain questioned whether or not he was still alive and if was being summoned for his final judgment. The long stretch of tunnel led into a cathedral. Glorious white walls sat under an enormous steeple made of wood and marble; architecture delicately crafted to create the stock heavenly atmosphere.

Twelve aisles of oak pews led up to an altar. Behind the altar was a giant pane of stained glass in the form of the Virgin Mary. Artificial light was passing through the glass and onto the altar as if God himself was watching over the ministry. A choir riser stood at one side of the altar and an organ at the other.

Bain walked down middle aisle of ruby carpet toward the altar. Although he felt as if he was alone, the congregants gathered from one end of the hall to the next suggested otherwise. Each pew was full of elegantly dressed believers, perfectly still and holding books of hymns. Some sat, some kneeled. All lifeless, yet excellently lifelike.

The mass of dead followers joined in celebration of a baptism. As Bain grew closer to the altar he could see a preacher, weighed down in enriched and embroidered cloth, with his hands dipped in a silver tub. Two very young altar boys stood at each side of the priest. One of the boys held a canister of fresh, burning incense. The choir was frozen in mid-song with the back of their throats showing as they belted out the silent note. Everyone looked excellently groomed and enthusiastic in their worship. As Bain gazed over the choir, a metallic clinking sound came from the far back of the cathedral. Bain turned, pointing his weapon. Yet he saw nothing. Everything and everyone remained mute.

He pushed toward the altar to get a closer look at the silver tub. He had to. He was compelled and there was nothing in the way to stop him. As he inched forward, the details of the priest's face came into view. His eyes were solid white and sat deeply in the wrinkled sockets of the old priest's face. His robe was immaculately clean and his holy jewelry polished to a shine. Bain peered inside the silver tub.

A newborn baby lay drowned in a pool of thin blood with the priest's hands squeezing its throat.

"Dear God!"

Had Bain not yelled, he might have heard his attacker approach from behind.

But Bain did not hear the attack from behind.

Neither did Alton; his attacker rounded a marble column in the Roman bathhouse and struck him when he least expected it.

Nor did Cari. She was assaulted as she admired the artistry of the dog fight.

And neither did Gar as one of the assumed false warriors came to life and struck him in the side with a primitive, but effective weapon.

The orchestra of screams that bounced off the walls sounded far too familiar for Kayden to ignore. He lunged forward, sprinting ahead aimlessly.

When he came to a wooden double-doorway, he destroyed the doors and burst through the splinters. The dark chamber he entered had furnishings of a workshop. Forged in the cave wall, an intense fire roared. Several wooden tables were set around the chamber. Knives, needles, thread, and pokers were set neatly on the table tops.

Oil drums sat at the end of each table containing filth and fleshy innards. Stacks of dried bone and hair were separated as part of an assembly line to create the handmade torches that were mounted against the walls.

After studying the workshop, Kayden realized that he was standing in the room where Ospi pieced together his art. Appalled like never before, he kept his eyes down as much as possible. The most difficult furnishing to study was the scant remains suspended from the ceiling by chain. He felt guilty for even being in the same room swarmed with so many dead souls, walking over dried blood and bone.

Tools of medicine, very familiar to Kayden, had been placed neatly on each table. If was difficult for Kayden not to compare his own preparations to Ospi's setup. He couldn't help but see the similarities of his profession and the so-called artistry Ospi had conducted. A keen eye for the human composition, detailed knowledge of each organ, location of these organs, familiarization with organ preservation, restoration and repair of skin, as well as many other concentrated understandings were required for both Kayden's surgical profession and Ospi's creation.

This realization made him sick with distemper. As much as he hoped to differentiate himself from the insanity, he couldn't deny the relation between the two professions.

Other than the rumble from the fire, the room was silent,

which led him to believe he was by himself as he examined the room. But he wasn't alone.

From a dark corner, he heard weeping of a lady, almost childlike in tone.

He approached with caution. The dancing firelight showed him a young woman slumped on the ground. Her hands had been bound to a pole protruding from the ground.

Kneeling down at her side, Kayden gently pulled the girl's hair away from her face.

A sharp, mind altering dagger of confusion struck his heart, penetrating every inch of his soul. He wanted to shout and cry. He wanted this nightmare to end and for all his loved ones to be safe and sound.

Yet in that moment, he understood that the safety of his most cherished loved one would directly depend on his actions.

"Grace?" Kayden's voice was clouded with emotion.

The young woman looked up to identify who called for her. It was indeed Grace Archer. Her eyes went wide.

"Kayden, behind you!"

A roughly pointed fire-pick came straight for Kayden's spine. But with Grace's warning, Kayden was able to react in time. Using his thoughts, he jerked the weapon away from its user and shoved the attacker to the wall with enough force to bruise his insides.

It was a dark-skinned, dark clothed man that had tried to put down Kayden. He held a flashlight and had wrapped a rosary around his weak hand. The injured attacker hunched over on his knees.

"Kayden, No! Don't hurt him."

"Deacon James?" Kayden asked.

It didn't take long for Kayden to remember the secretive, awkward old man that served at his family's church. He spent many Sunday's staring at an altar where the Deacon had stood off in the background.

"Grace. Why are you here?"

Quickly and with his own two hands, Kayden released Grace's bindings and brought her to her feet.

"I came here to find you. I got lost... I'm so sorry." Grace embraced her only brother. She had never been so comfortable in all her young life.

"Do you realize how close you were to being...?" Kayden started to ask her, but couldn't bear the thought. He held his sister tightly.

Deacon James got to his feet, coughing.

"Dr. Archer, you have to stop this. Stop this all right now. You have no idea what you are doing." Deacon James pleaded.

"Yes. Kayden. Listen to him. He knows what he's talking about. You can trust him." Grace gave her support to the Deacon.

"Let us leave here now. Call the authorities. Let them take care of this," said the Deacon.

Kayden looked into his sisters eyes. In that moment, he realized that she was the only thing that mattered to him and he had left her behind. In doing so, he had jeopardized her life. Perhaps his quest needed to end. Nothing about the endeavor was right. He had been going about it all wrong. He wasn't a vigilante. A practitioner of medicine was his trade. Helping people is what he did. Evil would stand before justice somehow, someway. It wasn't as if he could rid the entire world of all the terror. That would take more time and power than he or any mortal man had.

Yet without question, he needed to see his face.

"I have to see him. I have to know." Kayden said and let go of his sister.

"No! You don't understand. If you finish this," the Deacon rushed his words, trying to explain something which required more time than he had, "if you kill this man. The world will die. All that is evil will have its way. Everyone, everything you love will die. You have to take my word."

Kayden frowned, assuming the clergyman had gone mad.

"The end of the world? You must be insane," Kayden said.

155

"Kayden, I know it sounds crazy, but look around. Look at you. There has to be some reason for it all. Maybe it's true," Grace added.

Kayden looked deep into his sister's eyes. He assumed the place had maddened her as well.

"Grace. This will all be over soon. I just want to find the old man and we will leave. Everything will be okay. The things I will show you. You aren't going to believe it. It's so incredible."

"No Kayden. Don't, please." Grace started to beg.

"Kayden. If you end this man's life. Grace will die, along with everyone else. Hell has bestowed a prophecy on the Earth. You are the servant of that prophecy. You have been blindly set on a quest crafted by evil. If you complete this quest, all will fall. In an instant, all that is light will turn dark. All that is good will rot. You must stop this. STOP THIS NOW!" the Deacon spoke with the most force he had ever used.

Their argument halted when one of the walls broke apart into two sliding sections allowing for an opening in the middle. Each of them took several steps back.

On creaky wheels, another statue was pushed through the opening.

Dressed in a dark trench coat, much like the dirty one Kayden wore, an upright crucified figure hung on a wooden cross with both arms and feet nailed down. However, the two arms were of different shape and color. The two legs were one of a slender women and the other of a muscular dark skinned man. The head of the statue was covered in a dusty, black drape that hung down to the floor to conceal the face.

From behind the statue, a metal prosthetic limb poked out just enough to join them, tapping against the stone floor as if to say hello.

With a tumble, the owner of the false limb rolled toward Kayden in an abnormal somersault, and ending the maneuver standing tall right before Kayden on his one and only limb, spinning like a ballerina, smiling like a clown.

Ospi Gamule stood on his false, metal limb, grinning at the

three of them, giving them a slight bow at his waist. Grace could barely recognize the creature in front of her as being the same man that brought her there. That man wore a sport jacket, a straw hat and pants. The pale, zombie before her showed its bald head and wore nothing but half a pair of cut-off shorts, exposing this hairless, saggy-skinned torso. There was only a nub for one leg and the other was jammed into a geared, aluminum contraption that served as his only mode of transportation. Yet, with the help of a cane and his back, Ospi maneuvered around like a gymnast, graceful and proud. He held his chin high, as he stood on one mechanical leg, welcoming his visitors.

"May I present, the Crucifixion of the God Man," Ospi said loudly with his arms stretched wide to keep his balance.

With an open hand, Kayden lunged at Ospi.

"Don't!" Deacon James begged.

Ospi had predicted Kayden's strike and dove into a summersault, dodging Kayden's limb. Ospi planted his fists in the floor, then slung his fake limb around with enough force to knock Kayden off his feet. Grace jumped back. Ospi also retreated a few paces to regain his composure.

"This is how you treat your host!" Ospi yelled with a raspy tone.

Kayden was more irritated than hurt by the fall. He slowly came to his feet and stared down his opponent.

""Let me do it, let Grace do it. Let anyone do it. Just leave him be. Walk away from this." Deacon James continued to plea."

"From this?" Kayden barked back at Deacon James, pointing at Ospi. "You want me to leave this thing here, to carry on with this evil. Have you not looked around?"

"We will take care of him. We will make sure he is brought down. Trust me."

"That's so typical. Make him pay, huh? What should his punishment be, Holy Man? Five Hail Mary's? Ten? Twenty?"

Ospi laughed.

"Or maybe we should let him go to the crazy house, where we can restore his sanity." Kayden concluded.

"And who are you to be the judge? Who are you to play God, killing those who sin as if you are perfection? As if you are the sword of our God?" Deacon James bit back.

Kayden paused. For the first time in a long while, a preacher's words clicked with him. Grace walked to her brother's side and looked up to his teary eyes with her own terrified appearance. She held his hand.

"Let's go home. Let's go home to Mom," she said.

The anger flushed back into Kayden's face.

"It is for our mother that I am here," Kayden stated, boldly.

This confused Grace.

Kayden let go of Grace's hand and walked to stand only a pace away from Ospi.

"It was this man that took my mother's body by force. How she did not instantly die by the mere sight of his filth is a mystery to me. It is from this man's seed, that I was born."

Grace nearly fainted in shock. The Deacon was not surprised at all.

"I was born of this man's violence."

Looking at his true, biological father, Kayden saw no trace of family resemblance. Yet, he could not deny his own blood. The similarities of their professions led Kayden to realize the one characteristic that had been passed on from father to son: the interest in the human anatomy. Ever since he was a child, Kayden had found interest in injuries, defects, muscle development and repair, sickness, and medication. Regardless of the polar opposition of their motives and end results, they were bound by their interest. Like father, like son.

Ospi sneered.

"Can't see the family resemblance, son." Ospi yapped.

"I do. I see it. All around me. That's what hurts the most. I see you in me," Kayden said.

"Well, aren't we the most adorable family?"

"You haven't a clue who I am, or who my mother is, do you?" Kayden asked.

"I've taken the flesh from so many, used it at my own will.

Dead or alive. I cannot remember them all. Perhaps, I did her a favor. Perhaps I did you favor by giving you life."

"You are a weak man. Hiding in caves, leeching on to big brother," Kayden added.

Ospi patiently replied, "I have something to be proud of."

Kayden could hardly swallow. His emotions had seized all his basic functions. He had to focus just to take a breath. "Like what?" Kayden asked.

"Why you, of course. I have created a God. A God with many followers with many different faces."

Out of spite, Ospi reached around to the back of the statue and yanked away the black drape covering the head. Kayden grinded his teeth and held back the tears he would eventually let fall the next time he remembered that moment. He looked up to see faces of his followers, Cari, Alton, Bain, and Gar. Their freshly dead bodies had been roughly sewn together to form a crucified man.

Kayden hung his head in shame. For the rest of his days, he would have an image to register in his mind. He had led a group of good hearted individuals, bound together by their willingness to take action, to a horrid death. Because of his carelessness, they had been slain by his very own biological father. The one who made him. Every breath, every step, and every action he took was a gift from the monster that stood before him.

He could listen to no more.

"Deacon?" Kayden called for the preacher man.

"Yes Doctor?"

"Ask the Lord to forgive me. I was born of this man's violence. And he will die by mine."

"*No!*" yelled the Deacon.

But there was no hope.

Kayden reached out to Ospi. The crippled man flew into Kayden's grasp. Kayden locked both of his hands on his father's cheek bones. Ospi's struggle against Kayden's grasp was pointless. In seconds, Ospi's face began to redden. Then his skin began to smoke. His skin bubbled up on the surface. Shortly after, Ospi's face caught fire.

Screams filled the madman's workshop. Along with those screams, fire began to spread throughout. The tables, flesh drums, walls, and the crucifixion statue all caught fire.

Deacon James grabbed Grace and headed to the exit tunnel. As much as she wanted to go back for Kayden, the Deacon pulled her out of the fiery underworld.

Halfway out of the cave, they could hear Kayden screaming.

"He's burning. We have to go back."

"Keep moving!"

They raced out of the cave as every piece of art that Ospi Gamule made was engulfed in flames. They passed through each of the four exhibits: the Roman baths, the dog fight, the battlefield, and the cathedral, before finding a way out. Every inch of the cave burned to become a grave of ash and bone, lost for all time.

The instant Grace and Deacon James escaped the cave through the blazing tunnel, there was an explosion like a dynamite blast followed by a minor earthquake. It was enough of a shake to knock Grace and the Deacon off their feet and into the mud. Black, thick smoke rushed out of the cave entrance and into the air. For more than a minute, the two of them could see nothing but the sun trying to weave through the dark smoke and ash. Deacon James held on to Grace firmly. The heat was hardly bearable.

"Is this the end?" Grace asked the priest with an unexpected calmness.

The Deacon did not answer. He just held on to Grace as if she was the only thing left to hold on to.

Another explosion erupted from behind them. This one was followed by a thunderous, human roar. Announcing the misery, the cry rushed into the tropical terrain, nearly deafening Grace and Deacon James.

The two of them broke their embrace and sat up. As the smoke cleared from their faces, their mouths dropped as they forward onto what appeared to be a crater, nearly ten feet deep, that resembled an impact point for a bomb or meteor. The entrance of the cave was no more. Only the crater. And at the center was Kayden Archer, kneeling with his hands over his eyes.

"Kayden!" Grace called to her brother.

She rushed down the slope to him. Deacon James stayed behind and watched with caution. When Grace reached Kayden, she grabbed him and held on. His body shook like a naked man in the freezing cold. His sobs seemed to come faster than his lungs could manage. He was covered in dust. His hands were caked with burnt blood and flesh.

Despite Grace's many attempts to communicate with Kayden, he only wept. Deacon James eventually made it down to his side.

"What do we do now?" Grace asked the Deacon.

"I am not...I do not know," he answered.

Kayden didn't seem to hear the conversation.

"What's wrong with him?" Grace asked.

"If what I know is true, all that is evil now lives within him. There is no turning back. It's too late."

Kayden, still hunched over holding his face, wheezed in pain.

"We have to help him," said Grace.

"We have to help ourselves."

Kayden stood up fast, throwing his hands in the air. The Deacon jumped back.

"Take it back!" Kayden cried to the heavens. Immediately after, Kayden lost all his strength and collapsed on top of the dirt.

Grace tried to revive him, but there was no hope. However, she was able to feel a pulse in his veins.

"What now?" Grace asked the Deacon.

Tremulous, the Deacon looked around for the next move.

"Let's get him in the Jeep."

Grace and Deacon James dragged Kayden to the vehicle still intact and parked nearby. Lying next to a tire was Deacon James's rucksack that he had left behind before entering the cave. They laid Kayden down in the backseat.

"Grace. Listen to me carefully. You take this bag. It has money, maps, and a gun. You drive this Jeep as far as you can away from here. Away from everything. Take him to the sea. Take him to the desert. Take him to the mountains. Take him anywhere, as long as it's far away from here. The whole world is going to be looking for him."

"Why? Why do this? Shouldn't we try and get him help? Maybe we are not too late."

"I don't have a valid answer. My gut tells me that we need to get your brother as far away from harm as we can. Perhaps we can hold on to what good is left in him. I can't tell you this is the best idea. I can't even ensure your safety."

His words were not a surprise to Grace, but they were an indication to a fact she could no longer ignore: the man in the back seat might no longer be her brother.

Grace fired up the Jeep and put it in gear.

"Gregory, thank you."

"No Grace. Thank you. You very well could be our next savior. You have an unrelenting compassion for your brother, which may be what saves us."

"Will we see each other again?"

"When you get settled, let me know. But do not tell me where you are. Only that you are safe."

Grace conjured up the only smile she could manage for the Deacon before driving off down the muddy road.

MINION
THE DARK SON

THE VATICAN
2 WEEKS LATER

A well-shined banquet table stretched fifty feet long under a ceiling bejeweled in the finest artwork, inside walls trimmed with polished gold. At the table sat the leaders of Catholicism, the top of the pyramid: the commanders; the law makers; the only ones under God able to advise followers on how to enter the gates of heaven. They all wore thick clergy garb and were adorned with royal décor. Several of the rings and watches worn by the aged men could feed thousands of the hungry.

A perturbed assembly, they gazed into a giant flat screen showing updated news coverage. On the screen were riots and other acts of violence from one part of the world to the next. America, Israel, Saudi Arabia, England, Italy, and several other nations all were experiencing random breakouts of terror. Each nation was dispatching their armies to subdue the crowds. Brother Ryan, the youngest of the cardinals, still in his late 50's, stood and clicked off the screen with a remote.

"What we have now is obvious. A mixture of poverty, continuous war, and greed. The kind of greed that has drained our believers' faith in our Lord. The only choice our people have now is violence. Brothers, this is nothing new. What makes it unique, however, is the timing in which these revolts are taking place. Simultaneously, as if one match was struck to light the fires across the world."

The assembly nodded in agreement with the bold clergyman's steady words.

"Many of us have looked at the events in Philadelphia as a hoax. A misinterpretation of the truth. A clever scheme conducted by the intelligence community to distract the attention of the people. Yet, there are those of the cloth who believe otherwise."

"Please spare us, Brother Ryan," a member of the assembly demanded.

"Prophecy, my dear colleagues. Prophecy is what it has been called. Yes, only a handful has speculated, but we should all keep our ears and our minds open to such theory. We must listen to what is being said."

"We have heard all that is needed brother. Let us move on to different matters, shall we?"

"Humor me if you will, brothers. All I ask is for your clear conscious. I have invited a leader of St. Matthew's Parish in Philadelphia to speak with us this morning. He has previously requested access to the Vatican archives. It is my recommendation to honor his request," Ryan pleaded.

"Why should we? Why open the doors to the complete words of our Lord? Why preserve them at all if we are to let any altar boy defile them?"

"This is no altar boy. This is a student of the Lord's word. Perhaps a more versed student than anyone at this table. And...," he paused to catch his breath, "one of the few that has worshipped in the same house as Dr. Kayden Archer, whose name you all have no doubt become familiar with."

Whispers and complaints spun around the table. Irritation and frustration became the topic.

The door at the end of the hall opened. Deacon Gregory James stepped into the room with his head down. He made his way to the end of the table. The assembly went silent upon his entrance.

"As many secrets as this place has, it's easy to hear what happens inside," the Deacon left his usual timid mannerisms at the door.

"Brother James, please. Honor us with your presentation," Ryan said.

"I thank you, but I have nothing to present. There are no...facts. All that I know, all that I have been taught, from the kindness of men to the capabilities of evil, have all been disproven. This place," Deacon James pointed his hand around the hall with a smile, "I once knew as home base, if you will. But now I see this place is nothing but glass. I see through it. And so has the world."

"How dare you insult the Vatican? If God has a home on this Earth, it is here. And certainly not any tax evasion like the one you bow your head in on Sundays," one of the seated men growled.

"You think this place has any power?" Deacon James asked.

No answer.

"This place will fall, just like everything else you see around you. We are moments away from becoming slaves to our adversary. Hell has the upper hand now. And it's slowly making its way to your door step," Deacon James added.

"And I suppose its Dr. Kayden Archer that is going to bring this terror to us. The wizard. The doctor transformed into a demon, who lifts chairs with his mind, who bends buildings in half and puts them back together, who makes fire without a spark. Is it this man who is to be our destroyer?" the seated man barked with sarcasm.

"Surely you are not implying that there has never been a prophecy within mankind. And the supernatural has never been exhibited to the masses. Isn't that what we have based our lives on? A prophecy given by the heavens?" asked Deacon James.

"Of course. Our Lord Jesus Christ."

"What's keeping Hell from forming their alliance with man to push their agenda? Don't make the mistake and underestimate our enemy," Deacon James shot back.

Another cardinal burst from his seat and pointed at the Deacon.

"This prophecy you have pried from the cold dirt is nothing more than a cleaver scheme fabricated by tired conspiracy theorists, yearning for a new story to sell to the crowd. It is all nonsense! There is nothing to support this theory. It's another false testament the Holy Bible and the word of God denies."

The tall clergyman's exploding frustration caught Deacon James off guard.

"What is it that you want?" another cardinal asked the Deacon.

He replied in a soft voice, "All that I ask is the opportunity to complete my research. To see if there is anything else to learn. To see if there is any chance in saving us."

"Have all the research you desire, good man. After you are done wasting your life down there, do the church and all its beloved followers a favor, and turn your back. We have other issues to consider rather than meddle around in demonic prophecy. There is one holy power that is capable of giving us his son. This is God. Perhaps this concept is too difficult for you to grasp," the standing clergyman snapped back.

Even with the insult, Deacon James was relieved, for he would walk out of the hall with access to the Vatican archives. He wouldn't even consider the fact that there were few alive that had been inside the Vatican Archives. All the journals and gospels not included in the printed and public Bible sat in these archives. If need be, he would study them all to obtain more insight on Kayden and Grace Archer's predicament.

As he marched through the maze of the Vatican's secret passageways, he held on to his cell phone. It was his only connection to Grace, who was losing her grip on life with every breath.

CENTRAL ANDES MOUNTAINS, CHILE

"We don't have to stay here. We can try another place," Grace offered.

With weary eyes, Kayden glared through the passenger side window of the parked SUV that Grace piloted. They had shut down in the most secluded spot in the parking lot outside of a mom and pop gas station. Although she offered to keep looking for a convenience store, one with fewer occupants, Grace suspected that there wasn't another store for miles.

But her brother did not answer. Instead, Kayden's full attention was held by the few pedestrians in sight; a man fueling his truck, the attendant emptying the trash, and the elderly woman leaving in her sedan.

As he focused on every move and gesture, his vision was replaced by an aggressive daydream, clouding his every thought, inhibiting him from concentrating on anything else. He saw the gentleman who fueled his truck, only several years younger, standing on his front porch kissing his wife goodbye and watching her drive away to work. In this vision, he shared the emotions of the married man. And as his wife drove away, Kayden watched as the man grew nervous, yet excited as another car pulled right up to the front porch. A voluptuous young lady bounced out of the car and ran to the married man. In seconds, they were on each other like animals in the wild, with no inhibitions whatsoever. Kayden had somehow entered the memory vault of the gentleman fueling his truck and found his sin—adultery. Not a single elegant, or heroic, or even gracious memory was offered to Kayden. Only the sin.

He saw the pump attendant in his youth, stealing a baseball glove from a convenience store. As the old lady in the sedan drove away, he met eyes with her. From her memories, he watched as she whipped a pregnant housekeeper with a belt for accidentally bleaching a bath towel.

Frequently arising, these visions were not from a first-person point of view, but rather as a spectator overlooking the act. Perhaps these were not memories at all, but God's records, Kayden thought. And even though the gas station offered some of the tamest, less abrasive, less horrifying sins he was forced to experience, it still ate at his heart and mind.

The three abilities he had been given after destroying Armand, Lance, and Donar had been blessings. The gifts had enhanced his person and made him abnormally effective in ways that man had never seen before. It had given him the control of a god. Yet his last gift, the ability to see the sins of those he came in contact with, had become his curse.

"Kayden?"

"I'm fine."

It was the first remotely positive thing Kayden had said to his sister for hours.

"Okay. I will be quick. Just a couple things and we're out of here."

Kayden nodded and Grace left the vehicle to run into the store.

Depression had overthrown his being. Planning, foresight, rationalizing were all basic functions he had thrived upon, but as he sat alone in that vehicle, his mind only allowed him to see torment, agony, sin, evil. He wanted nothing more than to sleep, or perhaps cut out the part of his brain that held these images swimming around in his mind. He hadn't committed this evil. He hadn't been an accomplice. Yet he was forced to experience these events as they unfolded as if they were actually occurring in the present. He felt all the pain it caused. He felt the regret, the stress, or even the pleasure of those who committed such sin. As he sat quietly, he slowly began to deteriorate from his mind out.

The instant Kayden burned the life out of Ospi Gamule, the first of the visions arrived. He witnessed murder upon murder and torture of unparallel magnitudes. People were cut into pieces and sculpted into decoration to construct Ospi's underground museum, and Kayden was forced to endure every step of the process. Yet, one vision triumphed over his mind amongst all the other wretched scenes of agony. It was the first foreign memory he had to endure and, by far, the most discomforting.

The vision was of a rape. Ospi and his brother Donar had forced their bodies onto a young, innocent-looking woman while their bodyguards facilitated. The woman was on a peace mission in Brazil to aid the poor and unhealthy. But when Ospi laid eyes on her, he wouldn't take no for an answer. This woman's name was Lauren Archer, Kayden's mother. And the rape Kayden had to witness was his very own conception.

A distraction materialized when a white SUV pulled in behind Kayden's vehicle. A clean-shaven, silver-haired man in his late 40's stepped from the driver's seat and walked around the truck to open the passenger side door. A stunning, Latin young lady stepped from the vehicle and wrapped her arm around her gentleman. As the couple breezed by Kayden, the silver-haired man shared a particular memory.

Onboard a private ocean liner, the silver haired man had his arm around a different woman wearing a colorful bandana over her bald head. Her skin was wrinkled. Her wrists were dreadfully thin. They both smiled as they looked out across the sea as the sun neared its departure over the horizon. The last few years of their twenty-nine year marriage had been difficult solely due to her struggles with cancer. Medical professionals had done everything they could to keep her alive and well. Some months were better than others. She would show signs of progress, only to be followed by weeks of hospital living and surgery. Yet even with her devastating illness, she pushed herself to venture out with her husband on an international cruise.

On the back of the ship, with no one around, the couple kissed and embraced one another tightly. With a radiant sunset before them, they stared into each other's eyes, smiling from ear to ear as if they had forgotten all the pain and suffering.

She barely felt her feet leave the deck before she was thrown off the back railing and into the icy ocean water. Her husband turned and walked away with haste, leaving his wife to be sucked into the frigid waters. At the mercy of what little strength she had left and the monsters of the waters, she gave an impressive fight for someone in her condition. But there was no hope for her. Just as her husband had planned, without her he could roam the earth as he pleased, funded by a hefty insurance claim for his deceased wife.

As Grace approached the counter with her picked items, the walls of the store convulsed, shaking things loose from the shelves. The cashier was clueless, as well as everyone else. But not Grace. She knew what was happening. After throwing plenty of cash on the counter, she rushed out of the store with the shopping basket. She threw the basket in the vehicle and jumped in the driver's seat. Kayden appeared to be harvesting enough pain and anger to explode as he rocked back and forth, breathing heavily. It was obvious that another vexatious vision had haunted his being.

Grace fired up the car and sped away from the store and on their way up the mountain side, as far away from people as they could get.

Consumed inside a sealed room securing miles of text and artwork, Deacon James buried his face in a handmade book mended together by thick thread. The pages were five feet long and thicker than leather.

Deacon James did not jump with joy when he found the original document of the Shudagon Prophecy. Before that moment, he was only familiar with the scanned copies floating around the digital world. At first glance, seeing the original text did not provide him with any unknown information. But seeing it with his own eyes gave him a sense of closure. And just as the rumors provided, it was written in blood. The bottom of the one page document was stained red.

Gregory didn't spend long studying the written prophecy. He had read the text many times. Instead, he attacked the shelves with haste, searching for anything related to the prophecy. After hours of research, his hope in finding answers began to dwindle. If the prophecy was true, he shouldn't have even been in that room. He shouldn't have been able to glance through ancient texts and adore the beautiful artwork his religion had supplied. Yet he still breathed. He still had his freedom. He was not a slave to evil. Yet, he felt the shadows gaining on him at every second.

Resting in his jacket pocket, his cell phone rattled against loose change. He had a voicemail. There wasn't enough wireless signal for him to check the message, so he was forced to pry himself away from religious history and check the call.

He exited the glass chamber and up a flight of stairs. When he reached the ground level floor, his phone let him know he had a missed call. Grace had phoned.

He didn't even bother to check the message. He called her back immediately.

"Gregory?" Grace asked.

"Yes Grace, it's me. How are you?"

"It's getting worse. I don't know what to do for him."

"You are doing beautifully Grace. You are a blessing to us all. We need you to hold on a little longer. I need more time."

"He can't even speak to me."

"The visions, they are getting worse? More frequent?"

"I don't know. I think so. Can you, maybe, come here? See if you can talk to him?"

"Grace, I need more time here. There's an answer in here. I know it. Besides, the fewer people that know where you and your brother are, the better. Trust me."

"I'm just scared. I want to help him. But he won't let me in."

"Keep trying. You may be the only thing that is keeping your brother human."

Grace took a deep breath into the phone. The Deacon could feel her distress.

"Grace, I have to keep searching. I will check back with you in an hour."

"Okay."

"And Grace. Like we spoke about before. If he seems to lose control altogether, you have to,"

"I know, Gregory. I know."

"God bless you Grace."

After hanging up the phone, Deacon James went back to his research, locking himself back up in the glass chamber of religious knowledge. He immediately went back to the original document of the written prophecy and stared. This time something jumped out at him. He focused a tight eye on the large blood stain at the bottom of the document. There were indentions in the smudge that looked like scratch marks to the naked eye. Something was underneath the dried up blood stain. Something more.

Deacon James went to the intercom system and mashed the talk button.

"Is there a photographer that I can speak with?" he asked the attendant at the other end of the line.

For the first time on his visit to the Vatican, he felt as if he may have found a promising trail.

Her finesse had abandoned Grace to the point that a task such as making a sandwich became demanding. The cold kitchenette didn't help. Neither did the plastic bread knife. The silence of the ragged cabin only forced her to focus on each movement, each breath, each turn of the buttered knife on the stale bread. She took her time, purposely stalling from going back into the living room. She only wanted to escape for just a few moments. But even his calm breaths kept Kayden close by in spirit. There was no escape for her. Not even for a moment.

After cutting the sandwich in half, Grace went back in to sit by the small fire where her brother remained fixed on the glow of the fireplace. He seemed to be in a trance. Grace offered the other half of the sandwich, which he wouldn't even acknowledge.

"After three days, I would be sure you would surrender to the PB&J," Grace tried her first attempt at humor in a few weeks.

Still nothing.

"Dad is even worse at making them. Too much jam. Breaks apart before you could even start," she kept on.

Kayden had made the weak fire without hands. After several minutes of concentration, he was able to finally get a spark. A couple of weeks prior, he would have made the wood roar within seconds. But it was Grace who had the energy to gather the firewood. A couple of weeks prior, Kayden could have gathered it with a simple thought. In the cabin, he could only sit and endure.

"Mom knows what she is doing. Hits the spot every time. Guess that's what moms do," Grace said then sighed, "Oh, Mom. I wonder how she is."

Kayden closed his eyes as if he tried to do a mental reset, and perhaps blank out Grace's words.

"I've been praying for her," she said, folding her hands.

After several moments of silence, Kayden's chime-in startled Grace.

"Don't bother," he said. His voice carried bitterness.

"Why? Why do you say that?" she asked.

"There is no one listening."

"I don't believe that."

"You should. It will save you time. It will save everyone time," Kayden quickly replied. His eyes never left the fire.

"How can you say that?"

"Because it's the truth. Let us hope that He," Kayden lifted his hands up to the sky, "is not paying attention, for his sake."

"For his sake?"

"Yes."

"I don't understand."

The fire crackled and spat.

"If God is paying attention, if he is seeing all of this, God owes us for an eternity. All the pointless agony, all the starvation, all the confusion, the lack of harmony. As each second passes, he dives further and further in debt to us."

Grace looked away. Gradually she felt as if the room had gained in temperature, or, perhaps, she was growing uncomfortably nervous.

"Gregory says it is we who have turned our backs on him. It is we who have made evil stronger than good."

"So God is weak and his people are traitors?"

Kayden's eyes left the fire and engaged Grace. His voice grew more fearsome with every word, yet he spoke with perfect clarity and conviction. He was preaching to her. The last few weeks had forced non-stop concentrated thought on the bare bones of humanity. *Why do we do what we do? Why doesn't God intervene? What is evil? Is evil the manifestation of human choice?* These were the questions that swallowed Kayden.

"Your preacher is a desperate old man trying to give his own life meaning, when in reality he has wasted every breath on a God that pays him no mind."

"Do you have a better explanation as to why you can do the things you do?" Grace asked.

The question shut Kayden up for a solid moment.

"If this prophecy is true, why haven't I transformed into some monster and wiped out the Earth? I can barely walk straight. I grind my teeth apart to focus on one pure thought," Kayden spoke to her with a surrendering tone, but quickly turned this around and spoke with power. "Regardless of the measures I have taken, I have brought justice to this world, which, in turn, will allow innocence to prosper. I have done this world a service. I have rid the world of evil when no one else would. As crazy as it sounds, does that even come close to describing the work of evil?"

"You can't deny the connection. How you were born. The four people you hunted down and killed. You can't just ignore that."

"One of the many stories the writers chose to leave out of the Holy Bible," Kayden mocked, waving his hands in the air. The fire seemed to jump start itself. The room definitely grew warmer. "Any supposed man of the cloth can compare any line from that ancient text to elements of our era. They do it every Sunday. You can take that story and preach it anyway you like. It's an open ended fairy tale that you can manipulate as you please. It's made a lot of money and put a lot of people into power."

"Your mother, who gave birth to you when everyone else told her not to, happens to believe in that fairy tale."

"Leave her out of this, please. She has suffered more than you know. If God owes anyone, it is her."

Grace didn't know exactly what Kayden meant by his reply, but she left the topic alone. She was losing him. As the conversation grew more and more intense, she felt Kayden's sanity crumble away. All that she knew of her inspiring brother was crumbling apart before her very eyes.

"Kayden, I know there is hope for you. You said it yourself: you have done this world a great service. And you still can. Ever since I was a little kid, you have always been my big brother who saved lives. You were born to shed light on this world. Don't give up on that."

"No, never again."

"Why not?"

"I wasted enough of my life as a physician. Cured murderers and rapists. Mended a few good people, only so they could kill themselves to pay the fee. My career destroyed my marriage. I spent all my time at work and only a fraction of the time with my wife. It's no wonder why she chose to be unfaithful to me."

Kayden's eyes slowly dripped tears. As the tears fell, he stared into the fire. Regardless of how harsh the fire became, it would not compare to the burning in his chest as he remembered the times he shared with his wife. Young college kids fooling around, carelessly. Young adults moving to the city, building a place together. Building a life together.

"I killed her."

Grace shifted her seat closer to him. She laid a hand on his back. He was warm to the touch.

"Don't say that. It's not true."

"I failed her and sent her to the wolves."

"No, that's not what happened."

"I've failed you. I've failed our mother. I've failed everyone."

The wood in the fireplace was bright red and hot as the sun. Grace nudged back away from the flame, at the same time, trying to comfort her brother.

"I have this power to do anything. Build. Create. Fuel. All I have done is pick off a few nobodies. I have failed."

"You can turn it around."

"I deserve to be damned!"

Kayden jammed his fists against his chair. At that instant, a gust of warm air blew away from Kayden. Both of the doors to the cabin swung open. The kitchen window burst into pieces. What little furniture the cabin held either toppled over or slid across the floor into a wall or corner.

Snow flurries rushed in the open doors and broken windows. Soon the warm air was replaced by the frigid, natural cold.

Kayden bounced from his chair and marched to the front door.

"Kayden, don't! Stay here! Please don't go!" Grace begged.

But Kayden did not listen. He left the cabin to wade through the snow-covered, mountainous terrain with little knowledge of his whereabouts. Before Grace could make it to the front door, Kayden had disappeared into the Andes, miles above sea level with numerous ways to lose footing and plummet to a certain death.

Grace wanted to run after, but she could not overcome the fright of the cold, the wind, the snow, and the height. Instead, she shut the doors and sat in a corner. There she cried out whatever tears were left.

Deacon James shaved days off his life as his old legs sprinted up fourteen flights of stairs. The roof was the only place suggested in the neighborhood to acquire wireless service. Yet he stuck his phone out in front of his face as he climbed the stairwell, praying for enough coverage to make a call.

He ran from a small, two bedroom apartment in a complex on the outskirts of the Vatican grounds. The dwelling served as a photo studio where a greasy, unshaven entrepreneur edited and printed shots for a living, and his services were well worth the half-hour the Deacon spent staring at a computer monitor.

Deacon James left the original document of the prophecy, which he stole from the Vatican archives, on the editor's large scale scanning device. He left his jacket. He left without paying the negotiated fee.

Deacon James shouldered a rusted, graffiti covered door to the roof. There he mashed buttons on his cellular telephone. It only took one ring before his call was answered.

"Gregory?" the voice on the other end asked.

"Grace! Where is he?"

"I'm not sure. Things got really bad."

"What do you mean? Where is he?"

"He just left. We finally talked. He's...so...different. So much hate. I can't even see my brother anymore."

"Grace, listen to me. You have to find him."

"He will be back. He wouldn't leave me here, all alone. Would he?"

"Grace, I found the final piece of the puzzle. I know what must happen for the prophecy to be complete."

"What? What are you talking about?"

"The ink stain at the bottom of the document, it covered

178

the final words of the prophecy. Something no one has ever seen before."

"Okay. What does it say?"

"The ultimate mortal sin. The one that trumps them all. Why didn't I see this?"

"What sin? Speak English, please!"

"The final words of the prophecy state the last task for Minion to take before completing his transformation. Grace, he must commit suicide. He must give up his mortal life by his own hands."

Silence on the other side of the world. The Deacon heard no reaction. No breathing. No crying. Not a sound.

"Grace? Do you hear me? He must end his own life. Then all will be lost. All will be finished. Grace, if you see the slightest indication that he is suicidal, you must take him down yourself. Do you understand?"

Still no answer. No breathing. Nothing.

"Grace!"

Deacon James yelled into the phone for ten solid minutes before giving up on the call. He fell to his knees and grinded his teeth in anger. Angry at himself for not ending this when he could have. Angry for the lack of knowledge. Angry at everything.

On the other side of the world, in the heights of the Andes Mountains, a cabin that had kept shelter over two troubled individuals of the Archer family was silent. The cabin was empty. And so was the gun holster that Deacon James had given Grace just in case she needed a dependable weapon.

Never had he witnessed such undeniable beauty. In all his days on Earth, there had never been a more immaculate example of nature's patient stride towards the heavens. Yet the only material that contained such allure was rock. Rock that had been pushed out by the migrating seas to form mountains of glorious design. Many adventurers saved their earnings, sweated through hours of ascending, only to experience the same sight. Yet the wonder of the Andes was only a far away background to the real picture of Kayden's reality.

His convictions were so clear that he might as well have shouted them over the cliff, deep down to the canyons, for all those who desired to hear a rant seeded by loathing and dejection. His heart poured out with a clarity he had never been so fortunate to establish in all his studies or labor or reflection.

Kayden preached to the still air, "All this can change. Pluck out the weeds. Cut away the poison leaves. Allow life to grow. Let innocence flourish. All I need is the will and a plan. All of this can be changed."

Yet as he spoke, he had to concentrate on controlling his own mind. The many visual memories he had collected never stopped pecking at his brain. As much as he wanted them gone, they were a constant, unpredictable distraction. He physically strained to push on with his rationalization.

"Take to the streets. Find food for the hungry. Build shelter. Rescue those in need. Pluck out those who cannot live by the moral laws of man. If they steal, take their riches from them and spread them to those without. If they rape, show the world their pain before they die. If they kill, they kill themselves."

Men, women, children being sliced in to pieces and hung up on walls. Men gunned down while they protected their families. Images of torture and murder dug at Kayden's focus.

"When the seas threaten the lands, fight back the waters. When the skies twist and turn, destroying the lands, ease the winds. When the grounds crack, steady them. When the air turns to poison, bring in new air. Where the soil is dry, bring water. Where there is death, bring life."

But it was the visions of his mother's violation that could not be overlooked. It struck his entire being like a spear to the chest. No clear, developed idea stood a chance with the image swimming around in his mind. Not for Kayden. Not for any man. Not even for God.

"But how? Could a crippled man run to save another? Can a blind man find the water to put out the fire? Can a deaf man hear the screams of the needy? I had my chance. I had the chance to change things. To end poverty. To stop the fighting. To end suffering. To let the world live."

"I ruined this place. I've brought confusion throughout the world. They wonder, why is this God here, taking out his revenge on his personal enemies? Why is this God not helping us?"

"Below this cliff lies the answer. The cure for all that I have done."

"Kayden!"

A desperate voice called to Kayden from behind. He didn't have to turn around to know who it was. There wasn't anyone else for miles that would find him looking over the cliff. Nor was there anyone in the country who knew his name.

But he couldn't face her. His eyes were bloodshot and teary. He assumed he looked like a monster. His sister deserved better than that.

"Kayden! Please come away from there. We have to talk. Please brother!"

"Go away now Grace. You need to leave me here." Kayden turned his head to allow his voice to break through the slight breeze that swam around the cliff side.

Grace shook as she yelled at her brother from several timid feet away. With the ground covered in day old snow, it was hard for her to get a clear view of the cliff edge. Luckily, with daylight and only a slight downfall of flurries, she could clearly see her brother's back.

"You don't understand. This is what it wants. It wants you to jump. It wants you to give in."

"Leave me Grace. Please. I don't want you to see this."

She took a couple of steps forward in her brother's foot prints and she folded her arms to retain as much warmth as possible. When Kayden heard her steps, he turned to face her.

"Please Kayden. Give me a chance to explain."

"It's too late Grace. I can't live like this. Please go. Go back home. Be with mother. She needs you."

Overloaded by pressure, desperation, and even guilt, Grace sobbed uncontrollably. She unfolded her arms and reached behind her back to her waist band. When Kayden saw her hand again, it held a pistol.

A comfort fell over Kayden when he saw the gun. He saw an end to all his suffering and all the suffering he had caused. The gun showed him the potential for pure darkness. No memories, no guilt, no murder, no rape. Only nothing. He silently prayed for Grace to conjure up the courage to point the gun at him and squeeze the trigger. Yet, after really considering the consequences, he couldn't let his only sister carry that burden for the rest of her days.

"You don't want to live like that Grace. You don't want to have to live with your own brother's blood on your hands."

"Come back to me Kayden. I need you. We need you."

Kayden's shook as well, but not by the cold. He shook by his agreement with his sister. She did need him. The world needed him. His powers were unique. His will was heartfelt. Yet his mind was no longer his. He could not overcome his lack of control.

"I can't help you Grace. I can't help anyone. I can't even help myself."

"Try Kayden! Try!"

Grace lifted the pistol a little. The nozzle was not quite pointed at Kayden, but threatened to do so.

"It's too late Grace. It's far too late. I had my chance, and I blew it. I can no longer control this anymore. It has to end, before I hurt someone else I love."

Grace jolted forward, stepping in her brother's footprints.

"Kayden, no!"

"I'm sorry Grace."

Without picking a particular direction, Kayden let himself fall from the cliff's edge into the deep descent.

Letting go, his mind was the clearest it had been in weeks.

He simply concentrated on the fall. He let his body tumble whatever way gravity desired. Kayden closed his eyes and just let everything go.

Spotted memories of his wife came to him. He remembered their embrace. Their kiss. Their simple touch. He remembered the little moments that lasted a lifetime. He remembered how those moments coasted him through the working days.

He remembered his crew. His followers. Bain, Gar, Alton, and Cari. He remembered the moments when they were all moving in the same direction. All reaching for the same goal.

He thought of his mother; a lady of pure faith and impenetrable love. She could have given up on him before his first breath, but she didn't. She could have spent more time on herself than on her family, but she didn't. Driven, faithful, loving. All the qualities a positive member of society should strive for.

His father, a man that took on the well-being of a child that he did not create. A man that provided the tangible resources needed to allow for a future for his family. That took courage, which he passed on to his children.

His sister. The intrigued, gentle creature he adored. She looked up to him so much, and all Kayden wanted was for her to be herself. Even as a novice in the game of life, she had some of the best rationalization and advice. She truly was the central adhesive of the family. Keeping everyone sane. Maintaining the love between everyone. Kayden thought, if only she had been a little more forceful, maybe he wouldn't have gone this far.

Cutting through the air, he heard his own name being called.

He assumed it was his mind fooling with his senses. These were the seconds before death. Anything was possible. Perhaps the last of his sensations were firing off.

And he heard his name again. This time closer. More intimate. More directional. Not as easy to ignore.

He opened his eyes. He saw the ground rushing up to him. A few more seconds and this would all be over. He turned his head and managed to tumble over once more to look toward the heavens.

But he did not see the heavens.

He saw his sister.

Grace had dove in after him.

Their bodies collided in mid air.

"Stop us Kayden! Stop us!" Grace screamed in Kayden's ear.

"Grace!" Kayden had no productive response.

Fighting against the air, she forced the pistol in her hand to Kayden's temple. The ground was only a blink of an eye before consuming the both of them.

"Stop us Kayden. We will both die!"

"GRACE!"

A single gunshot reverberated around the rock. The gunshot echoed around the mountains and into the valleys. It was like thunder breaking through the tough air, searching for all the ears within miles.

No one heard the gunshot. But in some small way, everyone alive in that moment felt it.

EPILOGUE

Fatigued and wearing eyes of amassed sorrow, Deacon James did not bother folding his clothes as he packed his luggage. It was late and he needed sleep, but his racing mind, constantly rewinding the last few weeks, wouldn't allow for a moment of rest. To his knowledge, the fate of the world relied upon one scared college girl in hiding. As to her location, he hadn't a clue. The fact that he couldn't come to her aid, ate at him. A well-intentioned idea to keep her location a secret was the worst mistake of his time, he privately declared. There was nothing he could do, except continue to phone a number that hadn't connected for the past eight hours.

Abruptly, a screeching, tormented noise poured into his room through the open window. It sounded as if two rotating metallic blades were grinded together to amplify the highest of audible pitch. The noise easily acquired the Deacon's complete attention.

Once the screams of a woman somehow harmonized with the shredding sound, Deacon James knew what the source was. The expected had arrived. From that moment on, all would change. All would turn red.

A crash, followed by dozens of glass windows breaking in the same second. The Deacon inched toward the window. He had no earthly idea what hell had in store for his old eyes. Walking to that window initiated his surrender. He had gone so far, but not far enough. The tough choices had been there to make, but he had let them slip. He would have to face his demise head on.

With his head stuck out of the window, he peered into the street below.

An unmanned street cleaner had driven into a parked car, jamming itself into the metallic frame, breaking the windows, slowly destroying both vehicles. A middle-aged lady screamed for help as the operator of the street cleaner lied on the pavement, shaking in pain.

Deacon James let his knees collapse hit the carpet beneath. This was not the beginning of the end he had expected. He would live, if not for a little longer.

However, he wouldn't sleep. He pondered an idea over and over as he tried to rest. A quote he had read from an anonymous work stuck with him.

It read:

'Courage is not the absence of fear; rather it is the mastery of fear. Acknowledging fear and allowing it to be a part of you is what creates courage. The drive to be courageous is faith. Whether it is faith in God, faith in yourself, faith in your loved ones, or faith in your world. If you disregard your fear then you disregard any faith, leaving you deaden and blank. Let your faith help you find your fear. Hold your fear. Conquer your fear. Allow your triumph over fear to transform you into a hero.'

When an envelope was slid underneath his door, he immediately went for it. He ripped open the letter to find a scanned black and white photograph. The Deacon initially assumed the photo had been manipulated, yet the clarity in the detail forced him to consider over wise. The picture was of a highly unique, massive rock formation within a mountain range. Standing at a height that seemed unreal, the formation looked as if millions of tons of boulders were dumped into a canyon and shaped to form a rock skyscraper pointing to the heavens. No earthquake could create it. No man could have built it. No machine could have fabricated it. Only God could have done it. Or a God-like man.

On the back of the scanned copy was a note: *If you want to see this with your own eyes, be out front in 15 minutes.*

Deacon Gregory James did not care who slid the note under the door. He didn't care what the rock formation meant. He didn't care where it would lead him. His only hopes were for a second chance to save what was left of his beloved world. Deacon James grabbed his belongings and left the room to continue the mission God had given him.

TO BE CONTINUED...

COMING SOON

MINION

ROOT

BOOK II
OF THE SHUDAGON TRILOGY

Lightning Source UK Ltd.
Milton Keynes UK
UKOW052045050312
188389UK00002B/16/P